JANICE HARRIS & JOHN JONES

The Journey

Subtle Lessons in Spirtual Awakening

Outskirts Press, Inc.
Denver, Colorado

The Journey
Subtle Lessons in Spiritual Awakening

Outskirts Press, Inc.
http://www.outskirtspress.com

ISBN: 978-1-4327-0795-8

Outskirts Press and the "OP" logo are trademarks belonging to Outskirts Press, Inc.

PRINTED IN THE UNITED STATES OF AMERICA

IN MEMORY

In Loving memory of my Mother, Marian Rosella Bratcher - Rochester, whom I will love for all of eternity; you've earned a much deserved place in my heart. Mom was also an energetic, talented writer. She always took an interest in those things that were important to me and taught me to KNOW and always remember that God resided within me; within each and every being. She taught me to look within to find the answers to all of life's questions and she taught me to love unconditionally; no matter the hardships one might encounter during this lifetime. Thanks so much, Mom, for your love, kindness, strength of Convictions, encouragement and guidance. Here's to you!

Jan

ACKNOWLEDGEMENTS

There are many people who gave the inspiration needed to hang in there to bring this book to completion. Without their encouragement and much needed advice, this manuscript may never have been made manifest. I would like to give complete honor to the Creator of ALL whose energy and light flows through me and because I recognize that "I AM." All others have my sincere thanks and appreciation, beginning with JB Jones! Thank you JB for taking an active part in the Actual writing of this Story. To my mind, we make a great team. Your brilliance is unmatched my friend. Thanks to my husband, David, our Children Shafta and Kenyesta; JB's wife, Beverly and their Family for their patience while our writing cut into family time and finally to all others too numerous to name, for the faith you placed in JB and myself that we'd fulfill our goals of publication. Thank you all so very, very much!

Janice

I too would like to Thank all those who were behind us as we wrote, discarded and wrote some more. Thank you Janice, "The Journey" was an incredible experience and sharing it with you was of the utmost Fun! And much thanks to all others who encouraged us along the way. This has been one unforgettable Highlight of my life and I am very grateful for the opportunity to be a part of all the sharing.

JB

CONTENTS

PREFACE

Peace, Serenity, Happiness, Knowledge. These are things we all seek in the search for answers of the Universe. We tend to look outside ourselves for these answers when in reality all knowledge can be found within.

From early childhood, society teaches us to focus on only those things which can be measured by Science or those things which have life by means of three dimensional or physical structures. Proof of this entire Universe and its workings must manifest itself in a way to be realized through the use of the five physical senses. Only recently has the sixth sense been acknowledged, but no real attention has been focused on this sense via mainstream society. The consensus is…if it can't be measured using the five senses or science…it doesn't exist.

Daydreaming is one form of "higher Learning" which can "train" one to focus on the inner self. Unbeknownst to many, during the period of dreams, we actually separate ourselves from the 3rd dimensional physical world and travel, quite comfortably, through the world of the Spiritual.

This story is to help facilitate and make aware the vast working of the human mind through imagination, the power many of us unknowingly tap into everyday. If you are one of those enlightened souls who can open the mind enough to think "out of the box" of the structures of the so called "normal society" – you will find yourself replacing the characters of this story with your own personal being-ness and the enjoyment found herein will awaken those sensations within the mind that have, before now, been asleep.

PRELUDE: INSTRUCTIONS

A beautiful light shines softly, as if through the mists and a voice speaks to whisper. It is neither male nor female.

"You have done us proud Whisper. You have anchored a place for yourself in the fourth dimension. But you have one more mission which must be completed before you claim your well deserved period of rest and reflection. Successfully you grew spiritually enough to cross the bridge from the slumbering unenlightened world, to the unveiled, enlightened world of wakefulness. Now you must make one final entrance back into the third dimension to be of aide to the next semi-awake soul seeking its way along the mystical paths of truth. The next soul is awaiting you in a diner in a small third dimensional town called Joppatown. His name is Jack Bonaparte Mitchell, Better known as J B Mitchell. You will materialize as a waitress, but you will avoid using a name just now. He is to be led to the wooden bridge just east of Joppatown in the forest. It crosses a deep ravine. You will remember. It is the place you were led to on your quest for truth. He will then make a decision on his own whether to cross or not to cross the bridge. Many before him have turned away. Fear limits the growth of most people. Only those who are worthy will step beyond Earthly limitations................"

CHAPTER 1
THE DINER

Whisper materialized back into the third dimension dressed as one of the waitresses in the diner. JB sat in a booth a few feet away from her, staring out of the window deep in thought ; a frown creasing his weary brow. He was tired…So very tired. He'd been searching a long, long time for answers to some of the questions that had plagued him since childhood. Many explanations were given to him as he grew to adulthood, but none had satisfied the deep, inner hunger for something more. There was something just beyond these physical boundaries….he was sure of it! Yet nothing researched turned up anything new. Nothing made sense anymore and he silently prayed for a greater power to guide him on his way. At that moment he became aware of someone standing next to the booth he occupied. Actually, Whisper had been standing there for a few moments now, studying the man before her. She knew the longing inside of him, sensed his loneliness.

"Hi Big Guy! Do you mind if I sit a moment? It's time for my break and the place is so crowded, yours is the only spot I see available." She didn't wait for a reply, but slid in the seat across from him. "It's none of my business, but I couldn't help but notice a sadness surrounding you somehow. I know the feeling. How many times have I sat looking out this same window? So many times, I lost count to be honest, until one day I found a way to change it all. If you'll let me, I'm willing to show you my secret". She smiled at JB and it was a winning smile, the kind that hooks a person instantly;

the kind of smile that puts one at ease automatically. "Look. I'm not in the habit of picking up strange men, but my gut tells me I don't have anything to fear from you and I think I can help. As a matter of fact, I know I can. We haven't been formally introduced, but sometimes things are better that way. I mean, I love mysteries, don't you?"

"Trust me. Today we change your life Big Guy. Let me make an excuse to the Boss and we can skip out of here!" Whisper hesitated. "You do have a vehicle?" JB said he did, amazed at the way the woman took charge. Amazed at how he let her take charge. Hell! He hadn't said one word during the whole conversation! She hadn't given him the chance. Besides……it could prove to be interesting. He didn't have anything better to do and for the time being hc didn't want to think about what direction he'd take next. Whisper returned and said cheerfully, "Lead the way!"

CHAPTER 2
THE BRIDGE

Awarding him another smile, she directed the pickup truck he drove in the direction of the eastern outskirts of Joppatown. She asked him how long he'd been in town and he replied he was just passing through. He asked if she was from this town and she cocked one eyebrow, grinned and replied...... "I'm just passing through." JB didn't press, sensing she'd tell him anything she wanted him to know in her own time, her own way. He'd just play along. Whisper reached in her pocket and lovingly stroked a crystal which would set the stage for a grand scheme of which JB would unknowingly become a part.

They had come to a place where an old road seemed to lead down to an old unused lane and she showed him the spot where he should park. It was well hidden from the main road; a perfect spot for a vehicle to be found sometime in the future. She suggested they walk. They walked through a wooded area in silence and then entered a clearing where before them stretched a long wooden bridge. Whisper sat down on the grass near the bridge, legs dangling precariously over the edge of the crevice. Fear didn't seem to be a part of her character as she stared out over the scenery apparently lost in thought. JB watched the woman, wondering if she'd forgotten he was there, but reveling in the peace this place seemed to exude. "Do you have children?" she asked suddenly. JB said he did and he described them one by one. There was an enormous pride in each description. She listened intently and smiled as he told her of some of the antics the children would use to have their demands met. Whisper then spoke to him in a soft voice, "I was just sitting here remembering them…..Children I mean, and my memory tells me they were the smartest little creatures on Earth at that time. Out of all the humans who inhabited this orb, the children were the most honest. Words that came from their lips could always be counted on to be pure truth. They never spoke with forked tongues. Of course, that was over a thousand years or so ago." Hesitating, she reached in her pocket and produced a beautiful, flawless, crystal clear orb about the size of an egg. "Would you like to see your children now?" She reached out her hand toward him with the orb resting in her palm. "Go on. Take it. It will transport you to where your children are right now if you sincerely want it to. All you have to do is ask with purity of heart." Whisper saw the puzzled look on his face and laughed so hard she almost fell over into the crevice below. A brilliant, unexplained light flashed bathing the whole area in a web of gold, but was gone just as quickly as it had come.

JB snorted. How dare this woman insult his intelligence. He wondered just what kind of game she really was playing here. Something was not quite right. It was time she did some explaining. He stood starring out over the ravine, the bridge pulling at his senses. "Yeah, right!" he said. "And I guess you could give me a really great deal on a bridge!!"

JB looked around. The woman was nowhere in sight, but he could hear her somehow in his head. Could sense her presence, could hear her, but….. Man! This shit is weird! Little did he know at that moment how much his life was about to change.

"As a matter of fact, I think I *can* give you a good deal on a bridge. But there are a few things I need to know. What kind of a bridge are you looking for and where do you propose to go? Just to toss a cookie in your cool-aid, you've already been walking on one bridge and it belongs to me," Whisper said with more than a hint of laughter in her voice. "You do, however, step rather mildly, as if holding back the strength of those biceps will keep you from falling through what you perceive to be weak boards due to the age of this bridge. Oh, but do I have a surprise for you! Long ago, and I mean thousands of years ago, I had the good sense to build using solid black Oak and where each piece is connected, the material that holds it intact is unknown to man. So step spryly my friend and use your psychic abilities to avoid all the booby traps!" Whisper laughed again and managed to say, "I love it!"

She continued when her laughter died away, "There was many a pioneer who thought he had what it takes to cross that bridge for a really great deal." She laughed again. "A couple almost made it, but at the last minute fear set in and that became their undoing." JB could feel the tug of the bridge before him and he wondered why something as inanimate as a bridge could have any effect on him. He could still feel the presence of the mysterious waitress he had picked up a few minutes before. Picked up? He was suddenly confused about the whole scene playing out before him. Where was she now, why could he hear her voice in his head and not see her? Where did she go? JB knew that people didn't simply vanish, but something happened to her. After a moment, he stopped to listen to the voice in his head.

"So, you want to buy this bridge, do you? Oh, but imagine the *priceless* value that would be placed on such an exquisite piece! Are you sure you want to pursue this endeavor? It would be like standing before Mount Fuji and having to be at its base on the other side within the next hour. Needing a guide, but speaking no Japanese. Besides, did it ever occur to you that perhaps you are not the only in-terested party hoping to acquire this beautiful scenic "TIME MARK?"

The voice that seemed to come from everywhere continued in his head. "Look around you at the lush, overgrown foliage. Smell the aromatic perfumes of the magnificent flowers that bloom all season long. Gaze at the delicate patterns of the butterflies and pay attention to the warm, deep colors in this place of mystery. Hear the hum of the insects and listening even more closely, the lilting melody of a woman's voice in song; a voice that beacons you forward into the mist of the waterfall just ahead of you on the bridge. Pay attention to the spray dispersing into millions of tiny crystalline droplets, backed by the gloriousness of the most majestic rainbow you've ever seen."

The mysterious voice from everywhere and nowhere continued, "Below are jagged rocks drenched with the blood of many victims. Still it takes not away from the beauty of this place, for it serves as a warning to those who would approach with less than a pure heart.

For if the heart is not pure, the rocks can be heard calling….. "Turn back! Turn back!" Are you ….sure….you wish to pursue this endeavor?"

JB looked back toward the bridge and was startled to see that out near the middle, a beautiful waterfall was putting rainbow mists into the air as it crashed onto the rocks below. Sanity threatened to flee as he tried to remember why he hadn't noticed it when he arrived with the mystery woman. Cautiously, he took a few tentative steps out onto the wood of the bridge. Convinced that it was real and solid, he slowly made his way across toward the waterfall, stopping just long enough to produce a cloth from his pocket to polish the ebony oak. It sparkled and gleamed and made his heart swell with appreciation to levels unmeasured. A new voice boomed in his head and seemed to swirl all around him. Colors sharpened and sounds seemed to tinkle and cascade all through him.

"So far there's been no attempt to stop your progress on the bridge. But we've been watching you. The cloth you produced to polish the ebony oak….**did not** slip by unnoticed and so we find you interesting. The unrushed momentum of your progress expressed your great care and deep feelings for this place you wish to enter. There's been no screeching of the hawk, no clearing in this tropical forest of the creatures that live here and so we say we are **impressed** and you must be allowed to continue your exploration, Jack Bonaparte Mitchell."

JB was startled to hear his given name, but there was more to come. The voice changed pitch and JB could literally see the next words shimmering in the air in front of him.

"Endure what you must endure
Learn what you must learn
Then teach what you must teach."

As he stared spellbound at the shimmering words hanging in the air, the voice continued, "There is a lesson to be learned in crossing this bridge. We could make you guess, but that would be cruel and you've earned better. We are beings of love and light. You have proven yourself to be of light. We applaud your diligent excursions up to this point. We commend the brilliance of your aura. It is truly a wondrous sight to see."

New words formed suddenly and the voice continued with a power that was like nothing JB had ever experienced.

"THIS BRIDGE CAN NOT BE ACQUIRED. IT IS SIMPLY WHAT IT IS…...THE WAY FROM DARKNESS TO LIGHT AND BUILT FROM WITHIN."

JB took more steps across the bridge until he could see the other side through the mists. As he began to wonder if this was all a dream, the mysterious woman's voice returned. "Now, my friend, can you not see the good deal I promised you. You, also, are a bridge. You are hearing sounds which seem much like OM chanting. You are wet, tired, and thirsty. But, at the same time, you are exhilarated by the rape of the waterfall you just survived and excited by what is yet to come. Enter the cave that you see through the mists at the end of the bridge and your journey will have begun."

CHAPTER 3
THE CAVE

JB couldn't believe his eyes because right at the end of the bridge was a black hole that surely must be the entrance to which she referred. Deciding that he was either insane or getting there fast, he ducked through the mist and entered a world of darkness.

The other voice suddenly returned and boomed inside his head, "Welcome Jack Bonaparte Mitchell! We sense you cringe inside whenever your full earth name is spoken. It is a strong solid name with a smattering of individuality which speaks of firmness mingled with warmth. It is a most worthy name and when on Earth you must bear it proudly and with conviction. Do not cut your power by belittling your being-ness in any way. When asked your name, simply say…. "I am Jack Bonaparte Mitchell. My friends call me JB."

"That is that and you have given full power to your being-ness, so that when JB is used, energy resonates from the Big Power Surge of the pure energy of your full name. Almost like a battery and re-charger. JB, the battery, can be used over and over and is quite alright, but know that every once in a while it needs to be re-energized with the use of your full name. It was the name chosen for you before birth and its sound is in sync with those patterns of energy scallion waves through which your body functions in this third dimensional time frame. REMEMBER this henceforth!"

"Now, we give homage to your success and say to you that only the highest honors are afforded you on this day. You have come through the most rigorous of initiations with LOVE, LIGHT, SERVICE, WARMTH, and CARING and we must also stress the heightened condition of your psychic abilities in getting you here. Perhaps you are wondering from whence does the sound of this voice originate. Relax, and in your own words, savor the journey upon which you are about to embark. But first we will allow you the chance to refresh yourself and to become adjusted to the darkness here. You will find this darkness much different from the kind of darkness left behind on the other side of the Bridge. You have left behind the darkness of the unlearned, the darkness of those still asleep to the realities of the Universe. In the far corner to your right you will notice bunches of grass tied loosely into bundles and covered with fur. You must thank the spirits of the plants and the spirits of the bears for lovingly providing a place for you to rest. Find also an earthen jug of fresh spring water to quench your thirst and fresh fruit from the vines of the forest to appease your hunger. You will find that the temperature here is exactly correct and comfortable. Your only duty just now is to eat, rest, or sleep. Someone will be with you shortly, to guide you on the next stretch of the journey."

As his eyes adjusted to the low light in the cave, JB had serious concerns about his sanity. Somewhere behind all the buzzing in his head and all the voices booming in on him, he kept saying over and over, "This cannot be real!"

He quickly toured the room he was in and found the things the voice had spoken about. He was surprised to find that he had no strength and needed a rest. His legs, like the rest of his being had suffered an enormous blow and the soft bed of grass and bear skin rug looked so-o-o inviting. Thinking that it would not hurt to rest a while before exploring more, he settled into the soft pile and relaxed for the first time in what seemed like hours. JB began reviewing the events leading up to this time in his head. Quest for answers, psychic readings, the first dabblings in tarot reading, talks with others seeking answers. The list grew long and one thing seemed clear, there were no easy answers to life's questions, but there were sure some strange ones. Sleep was slow in coming, but when it came, it was the sleep of the dead. JB did not stir.

JB dreamt of butterflies and strange, mystical places filled with beautiful people and magic. He returned to consciousness slowly and with a start, realized he must have been sleeping in that cave he had wandered into following some waitress. He opened his eyes and there in front of him, wearing a most revealing silky garment was the very woman responsible for his being here.

"Ah-h-h....., finally you have awakened to rejoin us. My Earth name is Madison Whisper-Blythe Solerro. I've been called by various different nicknames. My preferences, however, are Spirit-Walker or Jen, or whisper. And sometimes in my head I hear Jana, I don't know the reason why, but it is a persistent echo at times. You may call me Whisper. There are as many facets to my personality and nature as there are grains of sand on a beach or leaves on a tree or hair follicles on your head. I am ever changing just as everything in the Universe changes and knowing that there will always be change excites me."

"You may be wondering, JB, about the attire you find yourself wearing. The bulky clothing you wore when you entered these mystic caves had to be discarded and replaced with a lighter weight garment. The reason being is that we have many upward levels within these tunnels to travel to reach the Fourth Dimensional Realms. Your climb will be so gradual that you won't even realize the difference in altitude, but you will begin to notice that the density of your physical body will become lighter and lighter. Your heavier garments would have caused your ascension to become severely dangerous."

Slowly, Whisper smiled a sly smile and continued, "To keep you from embarrassment, I took the liberty of switching your garments as you slept. It saved you from embarrassment as well as myself, for you see, once I stepped into this space to escort you forward on our journey, I, by Galactic Law, am not now able to leave you. My duty is to escort you safely to that point of destination preset millions of years ago Earth time. So you would have had to change with me in the room and the ornery one that I am, I would not have turned my back to afford you your privacy. I would have, most definitely, exploited your discomfort. You can see that we might never have left these chambers." At this, she began to laugh to herself and her focus shifted to some distant place or event before coming back to the present.

Whisper regained her composure and began again, "The emblem on the tunic you wear will become clear to you later on. Try not to focus on it too much at this time. You may want to walk around a bit before we begin for although you can see the boots you wear, you will feel as if you do not wear any foot covering at all."

JB rose from his resting place and discovered that while he felt well rested, he was quite stiff and must have been asleep a while. He thought, "Just as well I slept here, this has been fascinating so far and there is a beautiful woman involved so it can't be all bad."

Whisper spoke softly, "I trust you are well rested? You have slept three days Earth time, though not one minute of Warp time. The spring water you drank was laced with an herbal formula specifically to make the physical body totally relaxed so that the journey ahead could be traveled in one quarter of the normal time of Earth. Did you taste anything as you drank? Of course you didn't! We *are* good, are we not?" She smiled one of her disarming smiles and the twinkle was evident in her eyes.

A million questions surfaced in JB's head, but before he could get the first one out, Whisper continued, "You may be asking yourself why I have been sent to guide you. I will explain that to you as we travel. But right now we must begin our Journey. There is a gold belt next to were you slept. Put it around your waist under your tunic. I wear a silver belt. You have learned already that gold is attuned to the male energy and silver to the female. Take my hand, follow closely until we are clear of this next tunnel. Oh, one more thing. I know that you have many questions, but do not speak until I have said that it is the time to do so. I must add, I am very amused at your state of perplexity. Come! We must depart exactly NOW!!! The portals have opened!"

Whisper took him by the shoulder and propelled him forward into seemingly pitch black darkness where the rock cave wall had been. JB was surrounded by darkness like none he remembered and stood still with his heart pounding loudly in his chest. He felt the space around him with his arms while waiting to see if his eyes were going to adjust enough to allow him to see anything.

"Can you hear me JB? Good. From this point on we will communicate telepathically. Hear me as I repeat again…from this point on we communicate only telepathically. If you speak using articulation and sound instead of the mind, we will be placed in great danger. I implore you to try to remember this."

JB, startled by the voice in his head thinks, "Yipes, I know she just spoke to me and yet I thought she was over there, but, but, ah-h-h........, ok, telepathy."

As the reality of this newest surprise sinks in, his mind wanders even as he tries to focus on what she is saying. "She is in my head talking. I must use it too? But I don't know how! Sh-h-h-h, I suppose mental yells are loud as well. Uh Oh, hope she can't read my mind completely", he grimaced at the thought.

Whisper's voice continues. "It is darker than dark here. Say to yourself that it is only an illusion."

By now, JB was used to voices in his head and was hardly surprised as Whisper continued. "There is a ledge which wraps around a steep curve and we are standing on it now. I am going to raise your hand and put it on a strong hold slightly above my head. Thank goodness it is no higher, but I surmise the Universe looks out for its own. When you feel the strong hold and your grip is firm, let me know telepathically. JB, I cannot stress this enough. Our continued existence depends on it. Do you feel them? Indentations just deep enough for you to lock your fingers into? And your grip is sure? Good."

JB couldn't help thinking, "I abhor this darkness and am so grateful for her comforting presence. I wonder if she is aware of the magic in her touch as she guides my hand to the wall. Trust, I must trust her."

The voice in his head resumes, "I am going to release your hand now and I warn you to be careful. I will show you why before we go farther. In a few moments you will see flashes of light, some more brilliant than others. Some will be colorful and will flash like fireflies. These are quite pretty. Then there will be flashes of blinding light and these won't flash very often, only long enough to light up this tunnel to give a quick assessment of the danger we are in."

"So that you aren't caught off guard and won't panic and lose your grip do as I say but VERY carefully. OK. Grip your stronghold tightly and then take one foot and move it backwards. Stoop slightly and feel behind you with that foot. Exactly. There is nothing solid behind you. I am taking a stone from my tunic insert. I am dropping it now."

JB listened intently in the dark, his ears aching for the sound of the rock hitting something, but only eerie silence comes from the cave. He thought, "Damn, there must be no bottom!"

Again, her voice is right inside him. "You are right again. If there is a bottom it must be miles and miles away. There is total silence here and my thoughts are like yours. It is bottomless. This is why I tell myself it is only an illusion. It is the best way to hang onto sanity. Think good thoughts and we will get through this tunnel uneventfully. Trust me."

"Trust?" JB nearly shouted out loud. "She wants me to trust her but we might be here until our strength is gone and we follow that rock!"

Her voice reassures him gently, "How long will it take? It is better not to think on this. Just think good thoughts and concentrate on making sure your grip is firm as we traverse these walls. OK. It's time to move, we've got to make the next Portal."

The darkness was overpowering, but JB was determined to see where this was all going to lead. He had already decided in his head that this was no ordinary woman and this was no ordinary cave exploration. He still had a million questions to ask as he concentrated on moving across the ledge.

"I know you are questioning why the need for silence, JB. Two reasons, the least of which is reverberation of the echoes that bounce off the walls of the tunnel and as we go on you'll see the comb sickles hanging far above your head. Sound causes them to break loose. They are a danger in themselves not to mention the overbearing noise that the echoes would make. Imagine our best musical sound system turned up to the max. The second reason is that there is a keeper of the tunnel whose mission is to allow no entrance to this passageway. I am told he lives in the depths. But it is the only passageway to where we need to go."

JB cannot help but think that if there is a being in those depths, it even now must be reading their thoughts and coming toward them in the utter darkness.

Whisper interrupted his thoughts with her calm voice, "Can he pick up on our telepathic communication? Great thinking, JB. I asked the same question. There are mechanisms within our belts that block the energy waves around our bodies, but leaves one channel open for us to communicate. There is a catch, however. We can be no more than 20 feet apart or all communication capabilities will be lost. We will be able to tell because static will occur in much the same way transistors in walkie-talkies react when the two devices are out of range of each other. If we get too close to each other the belts will cause a small shock of energy, which feels sort of like static electricity from clothes out of a dryer, to remind us so that you don't bump into me, knocking me off the ledge, or I don't stop short without letting you know, causing you to fall off the ledge."

He relaxed slightly as her voice continued in the blackness of his surroundings. "Precautionary measures have been seen to by our guides and protectors. They give us every chance for survival but the actual outcome is our responsibility."

From nowhere, a brilliant flash of light explodes through JB's eyes and sears the images of the ledge and the rocks in front of him into his shocked brain. The voice continues as if nothing had happened. "Oh! Here's the first burst of light. Lean as close as you can to the wall and don't look down. This will be my third time through this tunnel and I have never seen them hit the walls although some have come too close for my comfort. The light is actually laser energy. It can cut anything it touches in half."

It is somehow reassuring to JB when Whisper says the guides will protect them. He is trembling inside as the light bursts around them. He hoped she would be so occupied by the wall and the journey that she would not notice or hear his knees knocking. Actually, JB found the predicament he was in exhilarating and it filled him with a wondrous energy. He came seeking nothing and found so much more. Now if he can just focus on the wall a little bit longer.

His thoughts are interrupted by a strong message from Whisper. "Here comes a second one!" Softly, she continued, "I glanced quickly at your face to see how well you're holding up. This trek is intense to say the least. I was sweating profusely my first trip through."

His first thought was, "You were scared?"

"Scared? You bet! But you? You're actually enjoying this, aren't you? JB! LOOK! There are the color sprites. Magnificent aren't they?"

Swirling bits of colored confetti rose from the abyss and created laughing pictures as they floated along on the faint currents. JB could only stare at the beauty he could never have imagined. He smiled to himself and relaxed more as the show continued.

"Well, at least I know you'll be fine and I can relax now and concentrate on getting off this forsaken wall. You're sick. Anyone who has a look of excitement on their face at a time like this is sick!!! Maybe you'll meet the keeper on your way back through this tunnel. It is said he is the most grotesque looking being found anywhere in the Universe. That ought to wipe that craziness off your face!" Whisper frowned for a moment then said, "Great! There's the natural soft light ahead! We're almost at the end."

Tiredness was beginning to make JB's hands and arms shaky and he was so relieved to hear that the end was so close. He was beginning to doubt if he could last much longer clinging to this rock face. They dropped down from the precarious rock ledge onto a little shelf of rock that seemed to have a glow coming from within. JB realized that he could see fairly well, but there was no obvious source of light. It was a dead-end, no way out but back through that musty smelling tunnel.

"You were great back there JB," Whisper said with another of her heartwarming smiles, "but you have this puzzled look on your face. Oh. The wall in front of us? Yeah. Uh-huh. Well what do you suggest we do about it."

"What can we do about it?" he fairly shouted. "WE? Dammit, You brought me here so it is you that is going to do something!"

She was now grinning at JB. "OK! OK! Don't bite my head off. Relax Dude. You just came through the end of the world, you got both feet on the ground, both hands are free and now you panic?"

He relaxed slightly as she continued. "In about a minute we will have traveled through that tunnel exactly 1 hour and 10 minutes. Every 75 minutes a window opens here. So we have 5 minutes to enjoy each others company." Whisper laughed as she saw the look on JB's face change again. "Sorry, but I'm enjoying your discomfort again. Go ahead. Slap my face. Oh, but then you'll make noise, so I guess it'll have to wait until later. Listen. I'll try to answer some of your unasked questions while we wait."

In his current condition, JB could think of no rational questions, but the Keeper still held his interest.

"I did not by chance have the great fortune to see the keeper of the tunnel. I feel myself blessed, but then, I preferred to think that he did not exist. To think him would be to create him. Thought is manifestation. My free will was not to give him life."

JB saw the paradox she was making. If it didn't exist, how could he meet it later?

Whisper read his mind again. "What did I mean when I said perhaps you'd meet him on your way back? Well when our adventure together is over, I will have completed my mission for now. On the other hand, you will have to travel each event you and I have traveled together all over again twice more. It is part of the initiation of our worthiness. It is part of our schooling. We must learn first hand how to embrace life by not running away from death. Being fearful destroys many beautiful opportunities opened to us because we put into place those safeguards we feel will help us to avoid death, when in actuality what we are doing is teaching ourselves to be afraid of living our lives to the fullest. Each initiation we are put through here, teaches us to let go of the fear of living. Just relax and let go. Only then can we propel ourselves forward toward growth. We'll talk more on this later."

JB can't help but think, "I hate small cramped spaces. I hate the darkness and am so grateful for her comforting presence. The lessons she has to teach me appear to be more than I could have imagined with my old paradigms. Death still scares me however; not the actual act of dying, but the fear of missing out on experiences and teachings that fill my heart and head with wondrous joy." Suddenly, the rock wall in front of him began to shimmer and glow.

"Look!" Whisper yelled, "The wall is no longer solid rock. The portal has opened. Let' move. 30 seconds is as long as she lasts."

Whisper rushed headlong through the shimmering space on the wall and JB could feel her energy tugging him along behind her. He closed his eyes and walked ahead. As he passed through where he knew the wall to be, he felt warmth envelope him and was aware that it was suddenly very bright. He opened his eyes and was stunned to find himself in another world.

CHAPTER 4
THE FIGHT

"Sorry to rush you along so forcefully. I just didn't want to see you get stuck between two worlds. That would have been the ultimate nightmare!" Whisper was speaking telepathically as JB took in the sights of this new place. "It seems peaceful here, doesn't it? Beautiful blue-green lake, warm Sun. After the last ordeal this makes you want to just lie down and take a nap. I know. It's very tempting. Don't get too comfortable yet though sweetheart." Whisper stared off into the distance with an unexplainable look and then looked at JB with a really weak looking smile. It wasn't a smile of reassurance.

She finally spoke softly, "This is the land of the Mutant Earth Warriors. Remember how so many people turn up missing each year on Earth? Many of them end up in secret compounds in this region."

JB wondered aloud if this was part of the cover-up information he had uncovered in his quest for knowledge.

"Right on target JB. Yes, the Dark Forces know all about them. Well, some of those people have been subjected to DNA experiments which have resulted in an 8 to 9 foot tall half animal, half human army of what they call the "Galactic Star Wars Warriors." She spoke softly and painfully, "Yeah, you heard me right. Which animal of the wild four legged creatures in the forest would you choose if you wanted an outcome of something cold, calculating and vicious, something that would tear anything to shreds without a flicker of remorse or compassion - its base instinct to "Destroy." Your first thought may have been the bear. The bear though, is sometimes known to be gentle. Sometimes a bear will turn away from its prey, unless it feels threatened. No, this animal I speak of is the 'WOLF'. Now mix that DNA strand with those of humans with little or no love in their hearts and tell me what you've got. Exactly. Terror and mayhem. On the other hand, if you'll think about it for a moment, there is always something that comes along that is a little better or stronger. There is always that quantum leap. Take boxing for example. This may not be the best example, but it'll do. One boxer may be the world champion for a couple years or more. But, he "must" vacate that spot at some point for someone with a slightly smarter move or a totally different style which will then reduce the champ to a pathetic sniveling child where once stood this powerful deity of sorts. As I told you earlier there is always change in the Universe."

JB tried to digest all this new information and was startled when Whisper spoke up again. "I asked you to trust me. Do you? I can go no further until you reply to this last question."

"Trust?" JB thought. "I trust her. Why has it been so hard for me to let myself go and take that leap of faith that the Tarot talks to me about? And why her? Fate? The will of the gods? My own personal reality manifesting itself in lovely flesh?" JB spoke aloud, "I am not sure yet <u>why</u> Whisper, but I do indeed trust you, plus you have pulled my cookies through this magical hell-hole so far, so I know in my heart that I trust you."

Whisper looked at JB and stared deeply into his eyes. His are kind, warm, loving. Hers are cold. JB's gaze into the dark depths of Whisper's eyes saw something unaccustomed there. What is she feeling? What is she… "NO-O-O-O, Oh my God!!" At that exact moment she throws a knife directly at his heart. There is unbelief, sadness, terror, anger and unacceptance mirrored all at the same time in his eyes now. The knife stops just short of encasing itself deep within his heart and then falls to the ground.

Too stunned to even move, he thinks, "I should be dead. How can someone you love and trust your life to do such a thing? Should I run before she strikes again?" Hundreds of emotions and memories boil up to the surface of his mind in an instant.

His stance is strong, but confusion mixed with something else stirs within his soul. Whisper smiles warmly again and softly says,

"I love you, JB, and this had to be done. I knew in my heart you would pass this test also. If you hadn't, I'd have misjudged you and you would have failed. I beg your forgiveness if you can go deep within your heart to find it. My actions were necessary in order for you to "know" that my next statements are true. No other proof is needed. I know deep down inside that my decisive action will save your life.

JB is in such a confused state that he barely hears what she is saying. Had to be done? Had to scare the be-jesus out of me and now she says it is for love? He struggles to calm his breathing and regain some small bit of composure, aided by the magnificent waves of love he feels pouring out of her and washing over his body; washing away the fear and replacing it with a peaceful serenity......lulling him into a warm and secure state, not wanting to hear the warnings in her voice, wanting instead to get lost in the emotions; to stay here in this lovely place with this lovely soul.

"The belt you wear places a force field around your body using Gamma Magnetic Rays infused through the crystal pyramids within our spiritual bodies. Nothing can penetrate this force field that your mind does not give access too. You screamed........No-o-o-o-o as the knife left my hand and flew in your direction. The belt responded to the stimuli of your minds command and the force field immediately activated. Therein lays your protection. I feel nothing but love for you JB. I am not your enemy."

"We have little time for chat," she continued. "This is important, so put aside your concerns and listen closely. **DO NOT** make the mistake in thinking that the mutant warriors feel any compassion for you because they are half what you are. **DO NOT** make the mistake of feeling compassion for them because you know they are half human. From time to time you may hear them telepathically cry out their anguish to you. That will be the human part and is part of their training. The Beast DNA strands are dominant. The Channel blocks of communication between you and me, through the belts, do not work here. I need to explain one more thing to you quickly.......uh oh, something isn't right here. I know we will fight before leaving this place this day." She whispers, "I can feel it."

Whisper screams, "Look!! The base of the trees!! Full of them!! In every direction!! We are outnumbered JB! Remember they can never outnumber you and I together, mentally!"

Everything is a blur as JB hears her screams and finds himself in the midst of a howling pack of animals.

Whisper is a dervish as she screams at the creatures surrounding her. The battle is intense and one of the creatures makes physical contact with Whisper. Whisper is breathing raggedly as she refocuses and continues in the fray. Blood streams from a jagged wound in her arm as she continues screaming and fighting the creatures that seem to be unstoppable. " I'm losing leverage! Get up JB! There's one on the other side of you! UMPHF!! Can't hold out much longer!"

JB barely realizes that he has a vicious tear running across his shoulder. Time seems to stand still as he looks for a way to defend himself and get through this nightmare. "Where can I get a weapon?" he screams.

Whisper yells, "We've got to use the new technology of the belts. The Force Field! Remember? The laser is in the power of thought from your mind! Direct it where you will! It will manifest through the eyes and out to your target! Let's do it!"

All conscious thought aside as he sees her precious blood streaming out, JB seems to be in automatic mode. As she screams his name, he feels some new power surge up from the very depths of his being. Power that scares him and yet is beautiful and sacred. Energy blasting in every direction as he feels the surge growing, becoming potent and sure. No time now, only the frenzy of the battle, the stench of fried flesh and the screams of the injured creatures.

Again, Whisper's voice is clear over the sounds of the battle. "We need more power! Don't give up JB!!! JB!!! Do you hear me?!!! We can do it! Trust me! We have to get close enough to each other to stand back to back and hold hands. Great! You are wonderful! Allow unconditional love to flow between us and these poor bastards won't stand a chance!" She screams like an animal as the fight intensifies around her.

JB could hear Whispers commands in his head and she quickly communicates a short set of instructions as bright light blasts in all directions. "Turn slowly JB. Now faster and faster and faster! Whew!! Look at those creatures fall under the blast of pure undiluted love."

As quickly as it had started, the battle was over. The stench was overpowering and burned his nostrils as JB tried to keep his bile down. Whisper is standing but bloodied. She is exuberant as she exclaims, "Whew! We did it! Awesome JB!"

As they embrace and kiss for the first time, he feels the same new power surging up again and in a flash of insight, recognizes it for what it is. Love. Simple, honest, love. No conditions, no control. Love. The very essence of his being flowing up and spilling over him and washing away the pain and hurt. She has his hand and is talking through the fog that is surrounding him as the energy of this unconditional love pours out and flows all around.

"I'd trust you any day to watch my back," whisper says with a weak smile. "Thanks. What do you say we blow this place and go where we can get some rest." She is breathing hard, ragged gasps as she says, "Face me. Now take one hand and place it over your heart. Take the other one and touch the circle in the center of your belt. Look straight into my eyes...." Whoosh! Thud. Thud. "Ouch!!"

"Oh man. Don't want to go through that again. But we can relax now. Sleep. We.......just......landed......through the next......window."

JB's emotions overwhelmed him and he knew at that moment that the adventure must turn inside as he is losing his grip on the conscious plane.…...sliding away toward...... "Hold me Whisper" ......slipping away......blackness envelopes his mind......

Out of nowhere the thought occurs to me that I must be dreaming. I remember falling asleep in the cave with Whisper and now this new nightmare is suddenly upon me. As I peer through the darkness, I become aware that I am not falling into blackness, but rather flying along, well above ground. I look down once again and I see my feet below me and nothing else. The same gripping fear begins to rise in my chest, but I can control it I find by repeating over and over, "It is only a dream, it is only a dream." I can begin to make out shapes ahead in the inky darkness and realize I am slowly descending closer to what appears to be an ocean with small islands dotting the horizon. I must be flying toward the sunrise because the horizon in front of me is beginning to glow with a pink and orange fire.

So, this is what Robert Monroe was trying to teach me with all those tapes. I suddenly can't seem to remember if that long ago time was even connected to this life. If this is it, then perhaps I can change where I am going and control this dream. Let's see, if I stick my arms out like Superman, Maybe I can ... nope, it seems I have no control and I begin to get a little tightness as I approach a large island directly in front of me. I think that surely if this is not a lucid dream and I have no control, then I will not crash, or if I do, I will wake up back in the cave safe with Whisper. Funny how even in the middle of this dream I keep thinking of her.

As I near the beach on the island, I notice my speed is quite slow and the sensation I had of great speed is gone. I drift over lush green foliage and smell the sweetness of a million blossoms in the air. The noises from below start to intrude on my consciousness and I recognize the sounds of many species mingled with strange unknown sounds. Again, I start to relax as I realize that whoever is controlling this dream is going to set me down in that clear area ahead next to what appears to be a magnificent waterfall. Suddenly, as if my imagination took charge, I find myself with sweet grass under my feet and a melodic roar over-riding the sounds from what now definitely appears to be a tropical jungle surrounding me. I can smell the dampness in the air and feel the fine mist brush my cheek.

As I walk toward the water to get a closer look at the falls, I can't help but notice that I am very tired and am falling asleep as I walk. Damn, this dream is just getting good and I want to keep going. I notice now that there is a walkway extending from the base of the hill next to the falls up into the jungle. It appears to be carved right into the stone. Upon closer inspection, I see that the water cascading down from above actually has a space between it and the rock face, and that the walkway, which is wide enough for me to walk comfortably along, disappears into the mist behind the wall of water. Again I feel a weariness creep over me and think of Whisper and how much I wish she could share my dream and see this sight. I have to rest a bit, so I sit in the soft moist grass beside the stone path and realize that I cannot even control myself...falling...asleep............

JB feels the ground underneath him and slowly crawls from the darkness back to awareness. He tries to rise, but the pain in his shoulder forces a groan and he nearly passes out. Whisper is close by and speaks first. "We don't need to use telepathy in this space. Great to work the mouth muscles again. How's your shoulder? Let me see."

JB rolls over on his side as she kneels next to him. "Oh God! You're burning up! We've got to take care of that and we've no time to waste. The bastards took a chunk out of you! First thing to do is to stop the bleeding."

JB realizes that she is also bloody and says, "But what about your injuries? You are our guide and need to be whole."

"Me? Well, my arm's a little swollen and bruised around the cut, but at least it's a clean cut. A little water and mud...I'll be good as new. Forget about me. I'm fine. It's you I'm worried about. You're a big guy, but you're losing blood fast! We need to get to water." Whisper thinks a moment and says, "OK. I know how to stop the bleeding for now, but I have to blindfold you. Sh-h-h, no time for questions. Thought you trusted me. I'll use the sash from my tunic."

Whisper securely ties the sash around JB's eyes and asks, "How's that, can you see?" By now, JB is beginning to wonder again what she might be up to, but he admits that he cannot see. "You're sure. OK. One minute."

Strange scurrying noises and a soft whispering swish sound are all JB hears. He asks, "What just made that swishing noise?"

"What's what? Swishing noise? I didn't hear a swishing noise JB. You aren't becoming delirious on me are you? Be quiet and save your breath. You may need it." Whisper smiles to herself, despite their injuries, and treats his wound. As she begins to bind his shoulder, JB can't help but think out loud, "Where did you get a bandage?"

"Don't worry about where I got it or what it is, love, just know that it is working. Here, let me help you stand. Put your arm around my shoulders. Its ok, I can handle your weight. I'm not a little kid 'ya Know!!! Sorry. I'm really worried about you. Besides, truth is, I *am* little compared to you big guy. Person could get lost in those arms. What? You don't remember tunics feeling like satin? Well now JB, did you ever really examine the material your tunic is made from? Didn't think so. Now shut up, a cave is not far from here.

We'll stay the night there." 'And then some,' she thinks to herself.

JB is not used to being tended by someone else and protests, "I'll be fine, let's just get on with this journey. No need to let me hold us up."

Whisper retorts, "No, you can't travel in this condition. I've got to clean this shoulder and then it has to be cauterized." He starts with the latest revelation and says, "I bet you look forward to that!"

Whisper, feigning hurt, replies... "OH, and I guess you think I *want* to do it! I won't speak on this anymore. Fine. I'll be stubborn or anything else you choose to call me." She laughs and says, "I've a feeling you'll be calling me a lot more names than these before this is all over and done with."

Hardly aware of the surroundings, they move up a hillside and approach a rock face along the side of the hill. It is impossible to tell how high the hill might be, but it stretches out in both directions before them.

"There's the cave. Little less than 100 feet. You'll be comfortable here." JB begins to try and untie the sash from his eyes as Whisper firmly says, "NO. The blindfold stays put until I remove it!" As they reach the cave, Whisper guides JB into the interior. A quick look around shows her that as expected, this place is already prepared for them with what they need for the moment. "Lie down on this Bed, JB, and relax as much as you can while I prepare for the next steps."

Whisper cleans the wound with water from a nearby fresh sparkling spring and dries it. She finds two large shells inside the cave to use as drinking utensils. From a pouch she carries inside her tunic she takes a powder substance and mixes it with water. A numbing effect is caused, but not so much that JB becomes unconscious or is pain free. It only makes the pain more bearable. Too much could be fatal. Then she drives two stakes in the ground near the midsection on each side of JB.

The noise brings him back to full consciousness and he asks, "What just made that noise?"

"Noise? Oh. Maybe it's rocks falling down the walls outside the cave. Here JB. I found some fruit on a nearby tree outside. I tasted it first. Unless it is slow to react, I'm still standing, so my guess is it's not poisonous. Not the best tasting things, but right now you need something in your stomach. On second thought….Maybe not. Not yet. I'll give you one in a few minutes, but drink this water. It tastes delicious. Good. OK. Give me your hands. No, in front of you. That's good."

Whisper takes two vines she had collected from trees in the forest and cut them in half. Then she ties a noose on the end of each piece. Four in all. JB holds both hands in front as he is asked to do. She quickly places a noose over both hands pulling tightly as she steps on his chest to hold him down, knowing he'd react against this latest un-lady like treatment of his person. She quickly leans over and wraps the other end of each vine around the stakes in the ground. Now the legs are a piece of cake. Straightening, she views her captive. Next she builds a fire while JB is rewriting the English language. She places a stone between two flat ended sticks and places it in the fire until the stone turned red hot. Then she leans over JB and placing a kiss on his lips, whispers in his ear….. "Love will carry you through to the depths of hell and then bring you back to me again."

With this, she places the hot stone on the wound on his shoulder. White-hot liquid fire shoots through JB as he arches his back and screams…….. "B-I-T-C-H!!" before falling into the abyss of obliv-ion……….

Darkness gives way to light and a distant memory of betrayal and hurt. JB opens his eyes and recognizes the beautiful waterfall and the walkway next to it. Iridescent mist hovers over him and seems to be telling him that the pain is not real, that this is real. Absent mindedly, he grabs his shoulder as the half-remembered pain from moments before fades further into the past. He thinks, "I know this is a dream, or I have died and been sent to paradise."

Slowly, he gets up from his resting place. He is instantly aware that he must see what is behind those falls, so he walks along the moisture slickened walkway toward the opening before him. Fear of the darkness and close places would have stopped him in another situation, but this is neither reality nor a dream. As a wall of living water cascades down beside him and crashes to the rocks below, he moves into the dark opening and stops to peer inside. His eyes are used to the soft outside light but it still takes a moment for him to ad-just to the shadows of the cave and to move behind the wall of water.

Immediately he sees that ancient erosion has created a room be-

hind the falls and it has not been neglected. There is a circle of rocks where a fire has burned recently. Low stones arranged to give the impression of seats and perhaps those shapes in the back are soft mosses to sleep upon. Ancient memories begin to stir and he tries to remember if he has ever seen anything like this before now. The roar of the falls is not nearly so loud here with the soft light filtering through the cascade of water. He wanders over to the fire and sits on a stone to ponder what is happening. Is this a dream? Is the cave with Whisper a dream? Is he losing his sanity entirely and making all this up in his head as the ambulance rushes him to the hospital to deal with the food poisoning from the diner? A million thoughts swirl through his head and he begins to feel relaxed. Like a child's game, he feels that the time of hiding his eyes is over and that he must cross the border between worlds the only way he knows.

Weariness has taken its toll once again and he slips to the floor to curl up and rest for a while as darkness overcomes him and he knows that the other world beckons again ....

CHAPTER 5
THE HEALING

Whisper looks down at JB, all the energy seeming to drain out of her body. Teardrops coursed down her cheeks as she took in the now blue grayish hue of the skin of the man lying so very still before her. She unties the bonds that held JB prisoner against his will and removes the blindfold, knowing very well that if she'd not handled this in this way, he would never have consented to the only healing method available to them. She places his hands in the most comfortable position she can think of and then sits next to him caressing his cheek. She says aloud, "Sorry big guy. How I wish there'd been another way. But, infection had set in and you were in danger of losing an arm or worse, your life."

She wiped at the moisture on her face well aware that even now, she could lose him. "No-o-o-o!" she screams to the gods. "Not this way! It won't end this way!"

Now water floods her face as she falls on her knees and then crumbles into a heap on the cave floor; her anguish apparent to all the spirits who'd occupied this space before them. "Whisper!" she admonishes herself, "How dare you give into despair. Suppose he were to come too and see you crying these silly tears. The admiration and respect you've seen more than once in his eyes would be replaced by revulsion and disgust. His trust would be replaced with uncertainty. Now is not the time to show weakness! I must never show him my vulnerable side; never let him see me cry."

A new resolve crosses the features of her face. This state of mind accomplishes nothing and it was with this thought that she remembered she'd removed her tunic earlier to staunch the blood that flowed from JB's shoulder. Face turning crimson, she quickly stares at JB and then down at her state of undress. Unbridled laughter erupts from her throat now at the thought of the expression that would surely be on JB's face if he were conscious. Satisfied that he'd be out for awhile, she snatched up her garment and walked to the spring to do the best she could to remove the stains from the tunic, then spread it on a bush outside the cave in the sunlight to dry. She fervently hoped it would dry before JB awoke.

Back inside, Whisper poured water from one of the shells onto the belt from her tunic and sat again beside her companion. She placed the cloth on his forehead praying desperately for the fever to subside. Though it was comfortable inside the cave, she saw JB shiver and knew she needed to cover him with one of the bear skins she'd seen by the pallets upon first entering this space. "I can do no more for him now," she thought, "but he'll need nourishment when he awakes." With that thought uppermost on her mind, she strode outside again and into the forest in all her naturalness, confident that things would work out just fine.

The Universe had blessed them. They would eat. She'd managed, though she was not real clear how, to snare a wild rabbit during the hunt for food. She'd found some wild onions and a few herbs with which to flavor the soup. She'd also found cat tails growing along the bank of the spring. The insides of cat tails are edible as are their roots. She'd toss these in too.

It was dusk now and the cave was getting cool. She needed to build another fire which would serve two purposes......cook the soup and heat the cave as well. She thought she'd seen an old turtle shell.......ah-h-h, there it lay in the corner, left here just for this purpose. The protectors were always one step ahead of them. She silently gave thanks.

After putting everything into the makeshift pot to boil, she decided it was a chance she'd take in going to the spring for a quick bath before the wild animals came out to drink. Then she'd return to dry by the fire and get back into her tunic before JB regained consciousness. Earlier he'd been thrashing and mumbling something about an ocean with islands and waterfalls and secret entrances.

Whisper hadn't a clue to where he traveled in his delirium. She'd had to hold him down again to keep his wound from reopening, thinking of tying his hands again, but he'd settled down and she was pleased now with the way he was progressing. He'd sleep awhile yet and he needed the rest. Not knowing why, a strong urge to kiss him entered her mind and she brought that thought to fruition. After all he'd never know. What *she* didn't know was that the kiss placed firmly on his lips brought JB back from the depths of wonderland to a light sleep. Feeling good about herself she left the cave, tunic lying on a rock on the other side of the fire.

She came back inside a short while later. Singing one of her favorite songs, she went to stand by the fire. The heat felt good. She wasn't aware of how she looked standing in all her glory silhouetted by the glow of the fire. Wasn't aware that she was not the only conscious being in the cave anymore until she heard...... "Whisper." Whisper froze. There was a roaring in her ears as she turned seemingly in slow motion in the direction from which the sound had come. Eyes locked, time stood still. Not sure how long she stood there, Whisper came back to reality with a jolt to her senses. In long strides she went to retrieve her tunic and could think of no way to gracefully smooth out her embarrassment.

"Shit! JB, you startled me." Pulling the flimsy piece of material over her head, she muttered, "Gotta get more wood for the fire." This was not true, however, for in the corner was a stack of wood she'd piled there earlier. Not meeting his eyes again, she left the cave.

Emotions out of control, all sorts of thoughts and voices going through her head, Whisper put her hands over her ears in an attempt to drown them out. She was wrongfully angry at JB for regaining consciousness so soon, but angrier with herself for allowing her guard to be let down. If she'd not learned another thing in life, she had learned to always expect the unexpected. The guides must really be looking out for this guy, she thought. He should have been out for the majority of the night at least. Oh well....what's done is done. Now she had to go back in there to face him. Perhaps the guides had decided to teach her a lesson. She'd exploited his helplessness when she'd changed his clothes early on and then had teased him about it. Perhaps this was a warning, reminding her to reign in her cocky ego and to be mindful not to abuse her many powers. That's a darn good man in there. Expert warrior, great companion. Never had she seen him lose his composure, except, (she giggles) when he thought she'd led him to a dead end when he was facing that rock wall. The only thing she could do now was to go back in and move on as though the whole thing had never occurred. She hoped she could get away with it that easily.

JB realizes almost immediately as she runs from the cave that Whisper is sensitive about showing her body. This knowledge mingles with the heat he was feeling a minute ago and he feels suddenly deflated. Surprisingly, his shoulder seems to be healing at warp speed and he attributes it to her magic and the magic of this place. He would have liked to think that the magic included freedom from inhibitions that they brought from the world they seemed to have abandoned. Perhaps he read too much into what transpired between them and was projecting too much of what he wants into each new event here. Be that as it may, he can't help loving her and having deep emotional connections to one who not only has saved his life but looks so darn good out of a tunic. Meanwhile, there seems to be nothing to do until she returns with more wood and her pride. JB resolves to pretend not to notice her when she comes back inside and perhaps it will ease her discomfort.

Whisper rose from the flat rock she'd been sitting on just outside the cave. She hadn't gone far. She'd left the silver belt inside near the pallet of furs she would sleep on. She was not so out of sorts that she wasn't aware of her safety, even though at times she could be a little reckless. She was mischievous a great deal of the time and many times she snared herself within her own web of games. This happened to be just such a time. Squaring her shoulders and taking a deep breath, she turns and walks back into the cave.

Making no excuses for not having any wood, Whisper walks over to the fire to check on the soup. It was coming along very nicely and would be ready for consumption very soon. Since there were only two shells which she'd used earlier for drinking water, she would make sure JB was fed first. Using one for soup and one for water, she smiled to herself and wondered if he'd drink water from her now. She was sure he'd be too weak to feed himself. She laughed aloud as the thought crossed her mind as to what she'd do if he dared to bring up what transpired a short while ago. Mischievousness was part of her personality and causing something to happen quite out of the norm was automatic. Pour the damned soup right over his head! Then he'd have no recourse but to come out of his tunic to have it cleaned too! She laughed at such a wonderfully entertaining thought. But of course she would not do this. No, she'd rather wait until he was back on his feet to pull something of this magnitude. She'd much rather match wits on more equal ground.

"It's wonderful to see you awake, JB" she said, using one of her most disarming smiles. "For awhile I thought I might lose you, but I see you've come through this with flying colors, just as you seem to do with everything else," she couldn't help adding. "How's the shoulder? Um-m-m, coming along quit well. I'm pleased with the looks of it. Healing remarkably. Do you think you can sit up if I prop some furs behind you?" Not waiting for his reply, she lifted him forward and stuffed furs behind his back. "I know you have one good arm, but would you like my assistance in getting some soup down?"

JB mumbled, "No. I can do it myself," under his breath and continued watching her closely.

"Fine. I'll get it for you since you're up to trying it on your own. I'm afraid there are only the shells used for water. You'll have to drink the soup and please be careful, it's rather hot," she added as she passed a shell of soup over to him. Picking up her silver belt, she replaces it around her waist and takes the other shell the short distance outside the cave to the spring for fresh water. Not running into any trouble by the spring she returned quickly enough to the cave.

"Is the soup too hot? I notice you've not touched it. What? Oh. Of course I'll take the first sip." Whisper purposely hesitates before drinking from the shell and hands it back to JB. Eyes twinkling, she stares at him for a moment. Then, clutching her throat, she widens her eyes and falls dramatically to the floor moaning and rolling from side to side. She dares a peek at JB and seeing the incredulous look on his face, bursts into hysterical laughter. She was laughing so hard that JB burst into laughter with her.

"This woman is absolutely insane," JB thought, but in that moment another bond had been forged between them.

Whisper began softly….. "There are some things I promised you

I'd tell you when the time was right. Perhaps this is as good a time as any. But before I begin, I'll give you this opportunity to ask any questions you may have. I warn you, I may not answer them all. There are some revelations that cannot, by Galactic Law, be revealed to you until the proper appointed times. We, you and I for now, are on a mission JB. A mission put into place thousands of years ago. We took part in the preparation for this very journey we find ourselves upon. We just do not consciously remember. You may find me infuriating at times Padre', but I'm afraid you're stuck with me until our agreed upon departure from one another." She begins reciting, almost like a singer:

> I AM YOUR FRIEND>>>.........
> I GIVE YOU LOVE AND MORE TIMES THAN NOT,
> THIS LOVE MAY CAUSE YOU PAIN.
> FOR IN ALL LIFE'S LESSONS ONE MUST LEARN
> WITHOUT DIFFICULT TIMES, THERE'S NO GAIN.
> TO SHIELD YOU FROM ALL THE HARDSHIPS OF
> LIFE,
> WOULD BE A BLOW TO YOUR GROWTH FOR SURE.
> HOW ELSE ARE YOU TO SURVIVE LIFE'S DANGERS,
> IF YOU ARE NOT AFFORDED THE WAYS TO ENDURE?
> DON'T ALWAYS THINK THAT YOUR ENEMY,
> IS THE ONE WHO ALLOWS YOU TO SUFFER.
> FOR GREAT HARM COULD COME TO YOUR PERSON,
> IF I WOULD ALWAYS INTERCEDE AS A BUFFER.
> SO WHEN IT SEEMS THAT I DO NOT CARE,
> AND YOU THINK I'VE ABANDONED YOU IN THE
> END...
> REALIZE, "PLEASE", THAT I SUFFER, TOO, RIGHT
> BESIDE YOU,
> AND REMEMBER THAT "I AM" YOUR FRIEND.

The last thing Whisper remembered were words spoken in the form of poetry coming from her heart and being forced through her lips. Most times when this happened she'd get the strangest feeling. A feeling of someone or something else talking through her and then once the verses were complete she'd feel completely exhausted. If

JB had started to ask any questions or to just plain talk to her in general, she would not have heard a word he said because in the next instant she was very comfortably asleep. That she had curled up next to JB would be a puzzle to her in the morning. A puzzle that would not disturb her in the least. Quite the contrary. She would rationalize her motives for doing such a thing in her own mind. It would make sense in her mind to get close to him for the body heat and for the security she felt in his presence and though she'd be the last to admit it because it felt good to snuggle up against him and it was a desire she could get away with by presenting the first two reasons to him if it came to that. Whisper wasn't above seizing an opportunity if it was to her advantage.

As Whisper softly recited her words to JB, he felt sleep creeping over him and knew that he was slipping away again. He felt comfortable and secure in the cave with her and was not even aware of the wound as he closed his eyes and darkness descended.

With a start, JB realizes that he is in the chamber behind the falls and is alone. He stands for a minute and tries to grasp some of what is happening to his world. Is he asleep now, or is this waking and the adventure with Whisper the dream. Confusion gives way to alarm as he notices that the fire circle is now stacked with fresh wood and there is a water bag hanging on a tripod next to the wall. Someone has been in his dream while he was away it seems. A thousand questions surface at this latest revelation and his head feels like it will explode. To clear his head, he goes over and sits beside the new wood and ponders this newest development. There has to be some rational explanation for all of this dreaming. Maybe it is the emotional upheaval he is going through after discovering that Whisper is more than someone he could kid about buying a bridge from, more than a friend who knows the parts inside he never allows to show. Tears begin to form in his eyes and he shakes his head to clear it. The emotions certainly seem to be on the surface today it seems.

Fire!! He jumps to his feet as he feels heat on his leg and stumbles over backwards because the fire is beginning to climb up through the pile of wood and the first warmth is already there. He thinks out loud, "How could I have not noticed that it was smoldering when I sat here...or was it? More clues that I am in a place not unlike my dreams, dreaming about a place that becomes more like reality every day. My goodness, if Whisper could hear me now, surely I could impress her with my insights and wisdom."

While I concede to the fact I've been trained to be an analytical thinker, nothing here seems right in my mind. The fire seems capable of taking care of itself. It freely gives heat and drives the chill from the stone walls, but it only creates questions. Who built it? Is this wood ever going to burn up? I feel very strongly that these and many other questions are going to be answered for me soon, so I begin to poke around the back of the shallow cave and discover that indeed, there is some soft moss piled to sleep upon. Maybe after I rest a few minutes, something that makes sense will come along and help me with this saga in my life............

All is quiet as I open my eyes slowly and see Whisper asleep beside me. I realize that the dream from the falls is part of what is happening to me and in a rush of insight I feel that it is there I will find the answers I might not get here. It is in that aloneness of the falls that I need to seek my inner self and communicate with myself on a new level. I look over at her again and wonder if she is dreaming and wonder at my calmness and the stillness in my heart as I begin to feel the emotions she evokes start waking from their slumbers. Now, I can feel them as live things inside me and know that I am learning to control them, to have dominion over the beasts of my heart. I notice her smile softly in her sleep and briefly think that she might be reading my mind, even now in her rest. Few things in life can be as rewarding as a softly focused gaze on a truly remarkable woman as she sleeps the sleep of the weary. Maybe when this shoulder heals (wow, I realize, it is not hurting!) we can explore further the reasons I initially followed her across that bridge to start this adventure. Holding these thoughts in my heart, I know it is far from over as I slide back down the pathway to sleep.... Oh whisper, thank you so much for sharing.... For making me a part of this tale.... For everything. I am dimly aware of asking Great Spirit to give me strength to be worthy of what she is teaching me as the darkness becomes once again complete.

Outside the sanctuary of their cave, the noises of the darkness continue. Sounds carried on the wind gently wash over the mouth of the cave and blend into the background. Small, simple sounds of the night, like pebbles sliding away down a rocky hillside......

Whisper woke to the songs of the early morning birds and to the stirrings of the creatures of the forest. She could hear the water as it trickled across the rocks on the hillside and down to the spring. It was cozy and comfortable and she could stay here like this forever. There was something else too, but only half awake, she truly didn't want to focus on what it was at this very moment. Coming more awake she tensed, hardly daring to breathe. Her head was on a shoulder and her arm was draped across a man's waist. How? What? She tilts her head back and looks into a pair of gorgeous pale blue eyes, a smile tugging at the corners of his luscious looking mouth. She was probably killing his shoulder. It was not the wounded side, but any pressure at all should have been murder to him. He should have pushed her away, but he hadn't. She reached up and touched his face and then buried her head back down into his shoulder, fighting those emotions that threatened to over-take her at any second.

"What is wrong with me," she screamed inside. But she knows, it's been a secret within her for a long time now. "Why can't things be simple in this universe. Why can't you give freely of yourself without all the repercussions waiting just around every corner. Why must there be *cause and effect* for every little thing said or done."

Whisper lifts up on one elbow. She takes her free hand and again touching JB's face, she places a tender kiss on his lips. She smiles at him then and asks if he'd slept well enough last night. She apologized for turning his shoulder into a pillow for her head. Then she struggles to a sitting position, hugging her knees, deep in thought for a few moments. She knew JB watched her. She knew also that it was now imperative to get back on their journey before she caused disruption and failure to the entire mission. She knew what awaited them ahead. He didn't. She turned back to JB and asked very quietly if she could see his shoulder. "We'll need to stay here until tomorrow. Try to move around some today if you can, but lie back down to rest when you feel lightheaded or tired. I'm going to go to the spring to bathe and on my way back, I'll get some of the fruit I would not let you have yesterday and some berries I saw growing along the borders of the forest. You're going to need to bathe also, but I'm not sure you should attempt that distance to the spring by yourself just yet."

She stood up and fell silent for a few moments. Reaching a decision in her mind, she looks at JB. "Can you sit up? Great. Now. Can you Stand? Careful. Good." Whisper put JB's good arm around her shoulders. "Let's go love. Move very slowly. The exercise should be good for you. If you need to rest or if you get dizzy, let me know. I mean it JB. I don't want to cause you to over do it."

JB wondered where she was taking him this time. She smiled because she knew where his thoughts were taking him. He probably thinks I'm going to toss him to the wild animals or something. She giggles aloud.

He soon saw the spring was not at all far from the mouth of the cave. Water trickled off a rock wall down into a pool surrounded by the most beautiful flowers. The water was crystal clear and you could see multi-colored pebbles at its bottom. It ran off into streams in several different directions. There was an opening of sorts in the side of the wall of rocks and water shot out from this opening in a spray, the sun catching the spray and turning this odd landscaping into a little oasis. It was surprisingly hot outside of the cave and Whisper helped JB to a flat rock which sat partially in the water. What she did next threw him completely off guard. She pulled her tunic over her head and walked slowly into the spring. It was deeper than JB had thought and when she got about halfway to the center, it came just below her arms, she glided under and began swimming in abandonment.

"Come in with me. I don't think you can get your tunic over your head, so, I'll help you. I guarantee you, you'll feel much better," she said smiling mischievously. "Trust me." After bathing, Whisper helped JB Back to the cave. "Will you be alright? I'm going to get us the breakfast I promised you earlier. I shouldn't be gone more than half an hour. Try to rest for awhile. You've got to be good and strong before we leave here. I'll tell you why later and I think you'll agree with me." Whisper turned on her heel and left the cave as JB lay down once again on the inviting soft bed of bear skins. Before he knew it he had drifted off into oblivion.

I realize with a start that I am back behind the waterfall and there is a vision of great peace and beauty fading from my mind's eye as I sit here next to the fire. A quick glance tells me that the fire has been tended well and looks fresh still. There is little else to see *and I get up to wander around and see how big this cave behind the falls really is and what secrets it might be willing to reveal to me. Over near one corner, I am startled to find a pile of what appears to be clothing in a bag. Probably someone who called this place home long ago left them here. I continue to explore and wonder why there are no real signs of occupation. I know there's a fire and a place to sit, but this is a perfect spot for many things. The weather seems perfect, the falls give the place an ambiance that people would pay big bucks for. I wander over to the discarded clothing and pick up the bag. It is crusty with minerals, probably from the water spray and has been here many years it seems. I carefully unzip the top and shake the contents out onto the ground. Hmmm… nothing remarkable here…some men's and women's shoes and looks like a couple of shorts and some jeans. Old and moldy to be sure, but still recognizable as clothing. Curiosity gets the better of me and I decide to root thru them to see if any "treasures" got left behind. The first thing I notice is that there is an old and very moldy wallet in the jeans pocket. It is difficult to get it out without it crumbling, but I somehow managed its extraction. I open it and at once am shocked to see it contains a driver's license and credit cards. Shit, it sure looked like this stuff was older than all that………I drop the wallet to the floor and feel a wave of nausea rush thru my whole body. Briefly I flash on the thought that my mind has never wanted to vomit before now. It simply has to be some kind of trick I tell myself…a joke my nightmares are playing on me. Maybe my mind is in a playful mood and wanted me to feel real panic, just to amuse itself. I stoop down and as the soft light filters thru the waterfall and enshrouds me in its soft blue luminance, I see that I was right, the name on the driver's license reads…*__Jack Bonaparte Mitchell__*…*

As my nightmare of my discovery begins to release its grip on my mind, I realize that I am still here in our cave. I realize that I am not sure when it became our cave, but it is. As my mind returns me some level of thought, I quickly review what has happened to me so far and try to find some little thread that will allow me to hold on to my sanity. Have I really lost my world? Is what I saw a vision sent to me showing me all about the present or is it just a dream that was sent to me to get me thinking? Hell, if they can bring Bobby back on Dallas, then it could be anything listed or something I haven't imagined yet! I decide to sit quietly and see what my guides have to tell me, if in fact they even know where or when I am. I imagine all kinds of possibilities, then begin to focus in on the one thing that has led me here. Whisper! All that talk about greater journeys and warp time when we were in the first cave across the bridge. Maybe there was more to it than I even imagined and this is my new reality. Nah...that kind of stuff makes great New Age books but it can't be this real. Sorta like I remember when I read the Celestine Prophesy the first time. It was an interesting story and they really made some wild conjectures for the uninitiated. In time, I did begin to understand those insights, so maybe this is another level of that kind of growth............

A sound outside breaks JB's trance and he glanced up to see Whisper coming into the cave with a huge, greenish blue leaf among other things that he couldn't quite make out. He found her intriguing and she held him spellbound as she walked through the entrance.

CHAPTER 6
ENLIGHTENMENT

Whisper returned to the cave carrying a gigantic leaf within which was various fruits and berries, enough for quite a feast. She'd also found a long piece of wood with a knob on its end and an oblong piece of petrified wood with its center hollowed out. She had plans for these and thanked the Universe for presenting them to her. She had found a rough stone which acted as sandpaper and used it to smooth the knob on the end of the long rod-like piece of wood and had then washed both pieces in the spring. Like a little kid with new toys, Whisper couldn't wait to put these new tools to use.

"Sorry I'm a little late, but I got caught up in the beauty out there." Stopping short, she stared at JB, a brilliant smile lighting up her face. "You've done it, haven't you JB? You've finally melded the mind with the spirit! You are glowing. Absolutely magnificent! When did you realize the transformation?"

JB stood up and stared at her as if saying, "The woman has really flipped this time." He said aloud in a tone he hoped would discourage any opposition. "Whisper, you're tired. You've been on your feet for two days. Rest for a while woman!"

Picking up on the authoritative tone in his voice, Whisper gently sits the food and other things next to the stones where the fire would be later in the evening. She struggles to not let the laughter rising in her throat escape her lips. Taking a deep breath she turns planting both feet slightly apart, arms at her side, hands balling into fists, face serious / chiseled, one eyebrow raised. JB wondered a little un-easily what was about to transpire now.

Bracing himself for a possible turbulent storm, he instead got a bright spring shower as she very calmly said, "Stuff it buster. I'm fine. Besides I just woke up a short while ago and our talk is way overdue."

She flexed and relaxed all body muscles, a smile gracing her lips. She took JB's hand, brought his palm to her face and kissed its center. Then she took her finger and drew tiny, lazy circles on the spot she had kissed. Releasing his hand she walked to the bed of furs they'd shared during the night and sat Native American style. She asked, "Would you sit with me?"

She piled furs next to the wall the sleeping pallet was against so that there would be support for his back and shoulder. Once she was satisfied he was as comfortable as he could be, she began.

"Awhile back I told you we'd climb to altitudes so gradual you wouldn't notice. I told you the reason for light clothes. I hinted to you about earth time not being that of Universal time. You've faced trials beyond your understanding and survived them, seen places more beautiful than you'd ever dreamed possible, and found faith in knowing you were protected by the guides and others beyond your comprehension. You have found unconditional love which flows like a never ending fountain and is more filling than any water you've ever tasted or any food you've ever eaten. I ask you, JB, how does your shoulder feel? Do you know at what point you lost your boots that didn't feel like boots anyway? And when you slept, did you go back to the cave where you began this Journey? Did you view that place from the air as would a bird and did you view it, in-side, just by thought and wanting to? Once back inside that cave your thoughts reminded you of the bridge you'd crossed to get there, but tell me….Did you ever go back across that bridge? Of course you didn't. Tell me; at what point did you realize you'd left the physical world as you know it for good? When did you realize the ascension process had begun? It's OK. I saw your acceptance as soon as I walked back through the cave entrance."

She continued. "I will have made, upon completion of my mis-sion to take you to the border of the fourth dimension, three trips be-tween the third dimension and the fourth dimensional border."

1) "There was my Initiation Journey, like yours now, from the third dimension to the fourth dimension.

2) Next was my solo Journey from the fourth dimension back to the third dimension to greet you and teach you the lessons I had learned, and

3) To deliver you to the fourth dimensional border using those teachings."

"You will make three trips total before you rest with me at the fourth dimensional border awaiting the others. Three. The key number is Three. As in the emblem on your tunic. A circle with the "3" in the center, a star above it and a star diagonally in each corner below the "3", forming a pyramid. These symbolize Life, Death or Ascension, and the Fourth / Fifth dimensions. The circle surrounding this signifies a never ending cycle of life and that all are contained in the one."

"There are seven people in our soul group pertinent to this mission. All must go through this initiation. You will teach the next person and so on down the line until we are all at the border of the fourth dimension. This is enough for now. We need to eat." With this said Whisper takes his palm, kisses it, and draws little tiny circles in his palm where the kiss had been placed. JB mumbled to himself, "must be some kind of symbol."

Whisper made juice from the berries using the tools she'd fashioned earlier that morning. Ripping a piece of her tunic and rinsing it in the spring, she placed this over the oblong hollowed out wood and it would serve as a strainer. JB watched with fascination at how she managed to, so easily, turn simple things into something now magnified. Using one of the shells, she piled it with assorted berries and using the wood with the knob on the end, pummeled the poor berries until they did her bidding. Pouring the mixture over the makeshift strainer again and again, Whisper stopped the process only after she felt it would be enough to serve the two of them for a couple of meals.

Promising to return momentarily, Whisper took the two shells and went to the spring to clean them and retrieve fresh water. She looked for, and found a long, slim, round piece of wood and carried it back inside with her. Pouring the water over the remains in the strainer and letting it sift through, she gathered the corners of the material and lifted it from the opening of their temporary juice crock.

Standing, she broke the long, slim piece of wood in half by slamming it down on her thigh just above the knee, but on a slight angle so that it would not break true. "Wonderful!" she thought. She'd wanted sharp, jagged edges. She would use this to score the remaining fruit and to, though crudely, slice them. She put the fruit lengthwise into each shell all around the edges, so that the ends met in the center. Then she poured juice from the crock into the shell. She opened the leaf so that it served as a placemat, the remaining berries in the center, and a shell of fruit and juice on each side.

"Wait! Don't touch it JB!" She runs from the cave and comes back in a matter of seconds holding a beautiful multi-colored flower from a flowering bush found at the entrance to the cave. She places its stem in the center of the berries. She laughs aloud at the look on JB's face and says, "Breakfast and lunch is served, unless you want some soup left over from last night. It's in a corner of the spring under a ledge so that it would keep until today. It's covered securely with one of those giant leaves. Wouldn't want uninvited flavoring added to my masterpiece."

Smiling, Whisper says, "You and I are gonna catch fish, downstream a ways, for dinner tonight." She arches an eyebrow and then watches him for a reaction.

They enjoyed the simple, yet delicious lunch. Fish were caught, cleaned and roasted in giant leaves on hot stones that night for dinner. The day zipped by and JB's shoulder hardly bothered him at all. They shared a wonderful day! Laughter was abundant.

Now it had gotten dark and whisper had become unusually quiet. JB looked at her, flames dancing in her eyes from the fire, staring directly into his eyes. He couldn't tell what she was thinking. Wasn't sure he wanted to know what she was thinking. But she *knew* where his thoughts were and she decided she'd let him know where her thoughts were. She smiled. "Let's go back to your 'some kind of symbol' statement." Whisper takes JB's hand and kisses his palm, and then she drew tiny, lazy circles on the spot she had kissed. The palm instantly heated up and began to spread throughout his body. She knew it was torture and she smiled because he had no idea what torture was, but, she was certain he would learn.

"As I kiss the palm of your hand and my skin connects to your skin," Whisper whispers in his ear, "a subtle friction opens your energy connection energy points."

Moving from his ear and talking normally now, she says, "what you call the drawing of symbols is nothing more than the stirring of those energies. Oh-h-h you're very aware of what is happening to you, but my intent is so powerful that you don't control matters at this point. I do. The magic of something as simple as this can cause your eyes to cloud over with excitement, can cause heat to run all through your body, can make the muscles of your manhood constrict with a desire so forceful that you no longer belong to yourself." She hesitates, then smiles, "You belong to me. You thought my running away due to that state of nakedness by the fire was because of some form of modesty?"

Laughter erupts from Whisper's throat; the kind of laughter which has its way of making another person very uncomfortable and wary. She is able to control it enough to say, "Well, I don't want to burst your bubble sweetheart, but the reason I left was because if I hadn't, I'd have devoured you. I left to spare you because I was barely able to contain the animal passions that had just at that point consumed me when you called my name. My thoughts were far, far beyond this space. So, my love, you've no idea how close you came, again, to danger. Never underestimate me!"

With a sensual smile she comes out of her tunic, lies on the pallet of furs and to JB's complete bewilderment and total frustration, falls asleep.

Whisper awakes first the next morning. Slowly she lifts the arm of the sleeping man lying next to her off of her waist. Then she turns so that she can watch him as he breathes evenly in and out. She hoped the bitter-sweet pain and torture she'd purposely put him through last night didn't prove to be too difficult. She knew first hand what it was like to burn so deeply with desire and yet not be able to satisfy those desires. It was part of the growth process, necessary for the place destined for them. She touched his cheek and a twinge of regret touched her heart for a split second; passing just as quickly. Whisper knew it was time for the next lesson and knew it would be even more trying than the previous one. She knew also that JB was an exceptional spirit and that he must learn for himself this very fact.

Covering his body with her own, she whispers in his ear, "JB. Wake up, JB. JB stirred from a most wonderful dream, opens his eyes and then closes them, wondering why being awake is exactly like being asleep. Confusion begins to cloud his mind because Whisper covered his body in his dream too. Not completely sure if this was a dream or not, he places his hands on her back and moved them down over her hips. Whisper laughs, rolls away from him and stands up. A mischievous sparkle in her eyes, she says, "JB we have to get moving. The sun will rise shortly and we have to be at the flat rock by the spring when it does."

Seeing the look of bewilderment on his face again, as she'd seen many times now past, she stifles a grin and grabbing her tunic and heading for the cave entrance, tosses it back over her shoulder as she says, " I'll meet you there." JB groaned and covered his eyes with his arm. "The woman is doing her very best to drive me insane. I'm sure of it!" he thought. "Got to get a grip or she may find she's the one in danger!" Rising, he smiles and shakes his head. "Better see what the WITCH is up to now."

By the time JB reached the spring, he saw, if he'd not known better, what appeared to be a Mermaid? "Must be imagining things," he thought. Before he'd completed that thought, Whisper walked out of the water. She shivered as she pulled the tunic over her head, smiled and stretched a hand out to JB with a subtle unspoken command, "Come to me." As if in a trance JB did her bidding, moving toward her, it seemed, in slow motion. Whisper's eyes glittered like a thousand jewels, a serene look of contentment and happiness on her face. She backed toward the flat rock behind her and without any willpower at all, JB followed, hand out-stretched to connect to hers. Just as she reached the rock, just as JB's hand rested in hers, the sun shone simultaneously on the rock and the couple standing before it. A beam of light too glorious to describe descended on the two and transported them to the next space in time called......**MYSTERIES & SECRETS** of love......

CHAPTER 7
MORE MYSTERIES

There was color everywhere. Beautiful colors, Unimaginable colors. There was also music. The most perfect music to anyone's ear. It was soft yet melodramatic. It teased the senses and gave a feeling of security and total bliss. Lights like fire-flies, similar to the ones in the first cave, but, if imaginable, even more wondrous. Thy seemed to be a part of everything and there was a sense of being able to taste them. The atmosphere was one which induced intimate desires like none ever before experienced.

JB closed his eyes and immediately lost himself in the moment, wishing he never had to go back to reality ever again. He opened his eyes to Whisper's smile. It was a soft, loving smile and she tenderly led him to a golden stairway which went "Down" instead of up. There was a mist beginning to swirl about the ankles and in time the stairs were lost to view. JB hesitated and his body tensed. Whisper knew what must be crossing his mind. She'd experienced the same fears that he was struggling with now. It felt as though the nothingness was about to swallow up ones very being and yet without guidance, where was there to go?

Whisper waited patiently to give him enough time to come to grips with what it was he "knew" he must do. "TRUST HER." After a long moment, JB visibly relaxed and Whisper rewarded him with a brilliant smile and stood on her toes to kiss him on the lips, walking forward now across a straight, narrow walkway. The walkway was also in gold and led to a huge platform. On the platform was a huge circular bed surrounded by 3 chairs and all were encompassed within a frame of a pyramid. JB looked at Whisper.

She spoke, "Yes JB?" JB stared at the picture before him feeling things he couldn't quite describe, yet he tried to put his thought into words. "The number 3. Life, Death or Ascension, the 4th / 5th dimensions. Am I on the right track?" Whisper hugged him and said very softly, "Yes JB, you are on the right track. Have you noticed how lightweight your physical body has become?" There was a look of horror on JB's face. Whisper laughed a mild tinkling kind of laugh, like crystal wind chimes, a very uplifting, happy sort of laugh. Different than JB had ever heard before. "I want you to not forget that the circle signifies a never ending cycle of life and that "ALL" are contained in one. You need to know that now and for what you will experience next. I want you also to remember.......I will be very near. Do not feel abandoned."

All of a sudden the fog cleared. This platform was in the center of an ocean of water and Whisper was nowhere to be found.......

JB looks around him. "Nowhere to go. Nowhere to go. Whisper! Why have you left me in this place?" But he receives no response from whisper. He falls silent and studies the scene around and before him. Panic begins to crowd his senses, but then he remembers Whisper's last words.... "Do not feel abandoned. I will be near." So he stands waiting. Five minutes pass, purposefully timed, to give JB time to completely etch into his mind all that he was seeing. It seemed an eternity, but he had learned to trust as Whisper had taught him.

Bright Light began to cover the whole area, brighter and brighter until everything was encased in what appeared to be white-gold, shimmering light. It awed the senses and filled the spirit. A voice spoke and, as in the beginning of the journey, spoke in the plural. It was neither masculine nor feminine, but very soothing, very assuring and JB felt very warm, secure and relaxed.

"You may be wondering why you are here, alone, and surrounded by an ocean. The ocean represents the infinite ocean of formless spirits and within its hidden bosom contains all that is, or ever can be. The three chairs serve only to imprint firmly within your mind the significance of the number Three. Whisper has already explained to you what they symbolize. But the number three "represents" the enlightenment, growth and fine-tuning of ones soul. It represents selflessness and a willingness to sacrifice for others. It causes one to be highly spiritual with intuitiveness beyond imagination and is the number of all that is holy. It is these kinds of people who deservedly wear the symbol which you find on your tunic and you are a part of a group of souls who wear it in this point in time and whose soul group totals seven."

"The number seven is the number of creativity, warmth, outstanding personality, wisdom, Spiritual attunement, mysticism, prone to have a far reaching and rare outlook on life, with an intellect unsurpassed. These souls also appreciate that the fine things in life are not necessarily those that consist of materialism and money. They understand the finest things in life are those things that can't be seen or touched."

"Those numbers above, melded together, presents us with the number one. The souls who resonate to this number are pioneers; they have courage, strength and are not afraid of hard work. They are not shy about doing things in ways that others have never thought to do. They are leaders, not followers, and they know how to reign in their fears. They know that there is no separateness, that all is a part of the One and from the one …. all draws its energy. These ones must, however, always run a tight ship where ego is concerned."

"The pyramid is to contain the focus of pure energy being released to the spirit. All that is needed to release its powerful energy is simply the thought that it is done. So be it!"

The waters around the platform started to churn. Like a rough sea; waves smashing and tossing to and fro. Voices. Many voices were heard and the sound came from within the water. As he contemplated the situation he found himself in, the water calmed just as quickly as it had when it changed to unrest. "There is definitely something not quite normal going on here," JB thought. He couldn't control the feelings of insecurity he was beginning to feel. Then he heard a splash on the other side of the platform. He turned to look behind him. Splash!! He turned facing forward again to where he thought the second "splash" had come from. JB rubbed his eyes.

Now he knew he needed rest. He was seeing mermaids again. Splash!! And mermen! "Oh God," JB thought. "Help me."

"Hello, JB. I am Garth. My companions and myself have been sent to give you a tour of the city of Aquarius beneath the sea. There is nothing to fear and you will learn much.

JB whirled around, stark horror on his face. Before him on the edge of the platform was a man. No, a Fish! A Damned talking Fish! Christ! He looked like Adonis above the waist and a big Bass below the waist. JB started speaking in tongues. Nothing he said made sense to himself or anyone else. Garth let out a bellowing laugh, clearly understanding JB's dilemma. "You are very sane JB. You must simply trust us." At that very instance a beautiful woman, no....Fish!!, swam up on the platform beside Garth.

"I am Tatya. I am very pleased to make your acquaintance, again." Her voice was soft, musical, and as beautiful as she was. Like crystal wind chimes. Like Whisper. "Oh my God," thought JB. "Back at the spring when I'd gone out to meet Whisper. Had I.....was she....A FISH!!! JB was truly alarmed now as his mind was rejecting each thought that came to the surface of consciousness. He struggled to keep from blacking out, nausea rising in his stomach.

Tatya reached out a hand and touched JB's. Instantly a calming effect took precedent over JB's fright. He stared at this....Woman??? "Come with us JB. You have learned to trust. Rely now on that new found faith. Faith and knowing will never let you down." She smiled the most beautiful smile and JB allowed her to pull him to the very edge of the platform and then reality set in as to just where he was. He looked at her as if she'd lost her mind? Did Fish have minds? JB screams, "Whisper! Help me!"

Whisper heard, but this was something he had to do himself. Her heart went out to him, knowing the anguish he must be going through. She was off in the distance swimming with another group of Aqua Humans. But she was not close enough for JB to recognize who she was. Garth would handle this. Garth always handled the unconfident ones.

Garth reached up, grabbed JB by the wrist and with strong muscles bulging, pulled JB into the water. Down, down, down JB went, fighting and struggling until he thought his lungs would burst from the exertion. Garth still had a firm grip on JB's wrist and was not about to release him until a depth of about a mile down was reached. Tatya, using telepathy, spoke soothingly to JB in a desperate attempt to calm him down. Control needed to be reached and soon because the frightened man might strain the muscles he needed for mobility and if this happened, the trip to the city would be considerably longer than it needed to be and JB would be in dire straits due to pain he would inflict upon himself! Finally exhaustion won out and Garth released JB's wrist. JB said to himself (or what he thought was to himself), "Now this is just freaking dandy. Whisper promised to be near me, I'm sure I'm dead and......she ....lied!"

Tatya, hearing his sad resignation said, "JB, you are not dead in the Spiritual sense of the word. You cannot die. You are, like it or not, in the circle of eternity. To live is the most glorious gift that the Creator could give to his creations. You have free will and are capable of your own creations. These are gifts of gratification that you return to the one who gave you life. With each wonder that you create, you enhance or magnify the glory of the ALL MAGNIFICENT CREATOR of all the Universes. You are but an extension of "ALL THAT IS". Won't you try now to create? What do you need in order to swim here? Think about it. How long have you been under water? You are hearing me and seeing me and you are seeing Garth and all the other Aqua people swimming with us." Tatya paused just long enough to let the information sink in. "You are shocked that I read your thoughts awhile back? Don't be shocked at anything you may experience. It is all a tapestry put into place by one with more power and magnificence than your mind could ever *begin* to imagine. Now what do you need to swim. Think the thought."

JB realized that telepathy was used here under water. He realized that he was still living after being under water, now, for more than 20 minutes. He was dropping steadily down, down. He had stopped his struggling awhile ago; had made up his mind to just give up. Now after listening to Tatya and remembering words she had *spoken* to him on the platform....Faith and Knowing will never let you down...., JB regained a spark of hope. He looked around him. He looked at Garth and at Tatya and he realized that he was the only soul without a tail. He thought, "I need a tail. Of course! I need a fish tail!" As soon as the thought had been released out into the Universe, his legs began to itch and to tighten. Bubbles began to form around them and it felt like little blisters were popping open all over his skin, from feet to waist. He looked down at what used to be his legs and groaned. He wanted to cry too, but reasoned it didn't make to much sense in all this water and a few of his tears might make the tides rise out of sequence. All the Aqua people laughed at this unintentional bit of humor. JB, with a puzzled look on his face of hearing the laughter and then the dawning of why they laughed, couldn't help laughing himself. The danger was over. He had willed himself to become an Aqua person. It was necessary to get through this space.

JB felt pretty good inside. He'd accomplished something that his wildest imagination could never have prepared him for. He looked up and swimming toward him was Whisper. She stopped just short of him, treading water with her hands and tail and eyes sparkling, smiled at JB and said, "Hi Big Guy." She pointed to a group of Aqua men and women and said, "I was always in that group over there. Always near by just as I'd promised. I could not interfere in your lesson. It would have been to dangerous for me. You could have hurt me without meaning to. You probably would have thought I was really going to do you in this time," she laughed.

JB understood why and his face mirrored happiness at seeing her and he gained confidence in himself once again. He was no longer among strangers and ....*she didn't lie*, he thought. Whisper laughed again. "No, I didn't lie. But know what JB? You've got to learn how to use your tail to propel you forward. It can be done one of two ways. Move the hips from side to side like so." Whisper swam a ways to show him. Then she flipped her body, tail over head and swam back to him. "Or by moving the waist in and out. Like this." She showed him the second method and came back again. JB had a blank stare in his eyes. She knew she'd lost him. Laughing, she blew bubbles in his face. "JB! Pay attention to *what* is being done, not to *who* is doing it! Laughter rang out from all the Aqua people. She demonstrated again and JB did his best to concentrate on the techniques used.

It was a merry time watching JB learn to use this new mode of transportation. All the Aqua people pitched in to help and the ocean rocked with laughter, fellowship and love unconditional. The men would console JB by informing him (in different ways), that women were just natural at using the hips. Their bodies were made to bring on the switching action. (The men roared with laughter) Men, on the other hand, always started out like someone just learning how to "drive the straight stick" for the 1st time, but with a little practice would have the vehicle purring like a kitten. It was a wonderful time. An "Aquatic Party" and by the time JB had finally stopped sinking, he'd made many new friends.

Whisper said to him, "I'm proud of you." Then she hugged him. JB tensed and looked down, a look of wonderment on his face. Everyone else began to swim away. Whisper, treading water, laughed and explained to JB. "It's a normal feeling. And you've discovered that sensations and emotions still exist without the male / female organs. They really aren't necessary. This is the most important lesson we all must learn. Isn't so bad at all, is it." she smiled. "Come on, we've got to catch up to the others. There is sometimes safety in numbers and we haven't gone down deep enough yet to avoid the deep sea dangers....."

Whisper and JB caught up with the others and soon all were traveling about halfway to the ocean floor. This was by far the most spectacular source of beauty JB had seen thus far. Flanked on all sides by the Aqua people, JB felt safer than he had since the onset of his journey. No sooner had this thought crossed his mind, a situation way beyond JB's expertise presented itself. Seemingly out of nowhere came a half dozen or so very menacing, very large Sharks. The teeth on these bad boys definitely warranted no wrong moves on the part of the Aqua people.

Whisper said to JB, "JB, don't move an inch. These bastards are blind as bats and the only way thy can detect you is through sound and motion. There are too many of us for Garth, Jayodri, and Teak to use the lasers. It's very probable that one of the Aqua people could be hit. Can't take that chance." At that moment a shark moved in JB's direction. JB's breathing was rapid and his eyes looked frantic. Whisper very gently, very slowly, reached and squeezed his hand and said, "Don't panic. Please. Even if he touches you. For the sake of survival...don't move. I will not be able to save you if you do." Whisper slowly let go of JB's hand and allowed the current to move her away.

The shark seemed to sense something odd here. The sonic sound waves were somehow different in this area. Around and around the shark swam, circling JB again and again. Bump! The shark bumped JB. Bump! Bump! All the sharks moved in JB's direction and Whisper called to him "JB, the sharks are sensing your fear. Change your thoughts to love for them, for us, for the Universe." JB said very weakly, mind paralyzed with fear, "I can't Whisper, I can't." "Yes you can JB. I'll be damned if we've come this far for you to give up now. Turn your head very slowly and look at me....I love you. We all love you. Return that love to us JB. We beg of you, love us in return."

JB saw the look of pleading in Whisper's eyes and then he looked at the others and found the same thing mirrored there. Instantly his heart filled with an emotion never felt before. He was so consumed with love that sharks never again crossed his mind. He dismissed them as though they weren't there and when the emotion had waned and JB was back to normal, there were no sharks to be found. JB asked, an incredulous expression on his face, "What happened? Did I pass out? Where'd all the sharks go?" Everyone laughed. JB said, "Sh-h-h-h, they might come back!" Everyone laughed again and Cerriko, a beautiful Hawaiian Aqua woman said, "JB, they won't come back unless you call them back with your mind. Back there a ways, directly after whisper told you there would be safety in numbers, the wheels in your head began to turn." Smiling, she continues, "You reasoned that probably it was due to sharks. And that's what you kept putting out to the Universe. You brought the sharks." She grabbed his head and kissed him long and deep. "Keep your mind on something else, OK?"

Everyone laughed and JB looked at Cerriko, an unfinished longing in his eyes, then with some guilt at Whisper to gauge her reaction. Whisper was laughing too and shrugging yelled over her shoulder, "Tatya, Cerriko, Wami! Entertain JB. He's letting his guard down because he's gotten too comfortable with me." Then she swam away, the other Aqua women flanking JB.

JB thought, "um-m-m-m, this is not bad at all and there is warm liquid coursing through my tail. Wonder what it is." JB didn't know that everyone else knew what he was feeling. His tail looked like dye was coursing intricately all through it and was flashing a neon blue. Ah Yes!! He was definitely enjoying himself.

Soon a magnificent City came into view. It was unlike any far fetched imagery JB had ever conjured up in his mind. It sparkled like diamonds, every color of the prism shooting out into every direction. The Aqua people swam to a floor that appeared to be made of glass. They swam right up onto the floor. A semi-warm gush of air rained from a glass ceiling. It's many faceted design far surpassed the beauty of any architectural design he'd ever seen or imagined.

CHAPTER 8
MYSTIC CITY

"Welcome to Mystic City, JB. We are sure you'll enjoy your stay and we look forward to seeing you here again and again. I am Wami and I will be your guide while you are here."

JB didn't mind her guidance at all. All these women were beauties. He wondered if they were cloned. No, they all looked different facially, but the bodies where magnificently chiseled. Thy looked like…well, they looked like…..Whisper's! All the Aqua people were just lying in the same spot they'd just occupied since swimming up onto the glass floor, laughing and talking as if that was all there was to do. JB almost asked why no one moved, then thought better of it since he was sure he'd find out soon enough. It didn't take long for him to find out. His tail began to tighten and the orgasmic sensations were a heightened assault on his already over-taxed brain. When JB finally came back down to "sea", everyone else was standing there enjoying themselves at JB's expense, unbridled laughter erupting from many. Whisper's eyes glittered mischievously, as she reached a hand down and asked JB if he needed help. Indignant and more than a little embarrassed he slapped her hand away and this only made the laughter more explosive.

JB stood and then laughing at himself said, "Man!, that was one mind blowing experience. When can we do that again?"

Garth bellowed. "JB too much of that could be very detrimental. You'd have no strength left for other things. Come, you've much to see. Wami will escort you first to the men's etiquette lounge."

Wami smiled at JB and said, "The men's lounge is just up ahead to your right. I think you'll find pampering like you've never re-membered receiving in this life or your past one. You'll be very re-luctant to leave when it's time."

Wami was a very deep, rich, chocolate brown with eyes like that of a trusting fawn. Her hair was black with highlights of wine col-ored tones. Her voice was soft spoken and mild. She moved with the grace of a feline prowler. "Once we enter and get you all signed up and into the system, I'll leave you in the very competent hands of Leora and I shall return for you in a couple hours Earth time. When you have been with us long enough you will discover that, here, time does not exist. So you may ask... how do we know when to go from one event to another? As you approached the city you noticed, I am sure, the prism of colors shooting everywhere. Well, look at the tops of each of these buildings. There are different color crystals encased in energy barriers. There is a central monitoring station which keeps a record of everyone's schedules here. This includes wake time through sleep time."

She continued to her transfixed audience of one, "There is a mi-crochip, so tiny as to be minute, that is placed just at the base of the brain. It works with the brainwaves and automatically we know where we need to be and when we need to be there. There within the microchip is a small crystal color board apparatus. One color of light within the apparatus will connect with the color of that particular crystal above the buildings."

"Your next question is....so you mean you are controlled by a microchip? No, JB. The microchip in no way makes us go anywhere we don't want to go. For example, there will be classes you will go to while you are here. Each class is approximately one hour to one and a half hours long. There are three classes, three times a week. Then there will be the cetaceans link up over on Mystic Crystal Val-ley. These link ups are everyday, in no way mandatory, however. Let's say you've finished class around 10:30 earth time. After class you are free to go and do whatever you wish. However, your mind will remind you via the implanted microchip of the Link up start time. The microchip serves as an itinerary of all events within a given day. You may or may not take advantage of them. Free will is never breeched. Knowledge is never-ending, ever changing. You evolve at your own pace here. There's plenty of time. Nothing *but* time. Ah-h-h-h, here we are. Leora meet JB."

Leora was, JB decided, of Asian descent somehow. He wasn't quite sure. He wasn't sure of too much of anything these days. But Leora sported almond shaped eyes and a petite pouty mouth. She moved with....'Geez'......all these women moved with grace but it was mixed with a power JB found hard to describe in his mind. All he could think was "Awesome!" for want of a better word.

"Welcome JB!" She hooked her hand in the crook of his arm and led him to a strange room. "Make yourself as comfortable as you can on that Cushion over there between the crystal bars. I am going to lower a crystal lens viewer in front of your eyes and you will tell me which bodies appeal to you most. Choose all the ones you like and then we will take those and narrow them down until you are satisfied with one. Next a body tube will come down around you and your body will be molecularly restructured to look like the one of your choice. Have no fear JB, you will still be you. We are just calling back your old molecules you left behind when you were younger. The people of Earth have forgotten that they have the power to do this exact same thing and so they age.

What happened next was mostly a blur. JB went through...

1) The rejuvenation chamber – Took 10 minutes
2) The microchip implant microscopic surgery – Took 2 seconds
3) The massage room – Took 35 minutes, 7 women sending him to heaven
4) The pleasure room – Took 30 minutes, seemed like 2 hours, 5 babes. Wonderful illusions that he could have sworn was real, that released pent up tension and he never physically touched anyone! Whew-w-w!!! What a life!
5) The mystic Fabric experience – took 20 minutes; shirt of a whisper gauze, hardly there. Form fitting breeches with a Lycra type stretch but they felt like they weren't there and in actuality they almost truly didn't look much like clothes. He felt wonderfully free. Unhampered.
6) The tress shop – Took 10 minutes, hair fell in waves slightly past the Shoulders, mustache trimmed, beard trimmed.

7) The tanning experience – Took 10 minutes, lasts 90 Earth
    days, Swallowed one pill.

Leora returned JB to Wami at the front entrance of the Men's
lounge, not forgetting to kiss him before she turned him over. Every
woman having the pleasure to meet JB, would kiss this man before
he left. There were no inhibitions here. Copulation is a primitive
mode which does not exist in this space. It isn't needed. Unconditional love is pure and it can be felt with a higher intensity than those
emotions on Earth, simply by looking into the windows of the soul,
which are the eyes. A simple Kiss or touch would place you in an
instant oasis. It was a miraculous feeling and it was insurance. He'd
definitely come back.

Wami next showed JB to his room.   All doors automatically
opened with a "swish" as they approached. Inside the room was a
holographic fireplace which made one feel comfy and cozy.   There
were sensors on the wall that when activated, almost anything was
your command.   If a forest complete with natural creatures was
wanted, instantly one touch would put you there, fireplace gone. If
you wanted to create a winter scene, holographically you could be in
a wintry forest scene or you could be inside, fireplace blazing and
snow falling just outside a huge seamless window. If you wanted to
see what action was going on at the different social spots anywhere
in Mystic City, a huge satellite picture tube would make you feel you
were actually a part of it all. If you wanted to make love, an apparatus which covered the eyes and ears would create a scene so real that
if a timer wasn't set before using them, you'd get lost in the imagery.
So if JB wanted to indulge in the old ways, it wouldn't be impossible. If you wanted a real companion you could enroll yourself in the
Galactic Swingers Club, but if you wanted no feelings of obligation,
it would be better to make your own temporary mate using the Wish
Chamber right within your room. You would tell the computer what
color hair, eyes, your body preference, what types of clothes, how
the voice should sound using a voice simulator. You could choose
whether you wanted a sexy voice or just a pal to talk to, etc. Press
enter and instantly that companion would walk out of the Wish
Chamber, disappearing completely once the time line, you would
have set, was complete. The food was amazing. The way to get it

was even more amazing. Two electrodes on each side of the head close to the brain, think the thought and you have your desire triggered through taste sensations based on memory perceptions.

Wami took JB to all the social clubs, the oceanraunts (Restaurants), the Cetaceans Link Up which was a highly gratifying way to communicate with the Dolphins and Whales. Technology was used to interpret what was said one to the other. Once the technical devices had been used over a period of time, some would no longer need to use them, becoming spiritually attuned naturally to their new aquatic friends. There was also devices that could be called on for protection in the very unlikely situation of a Shark attack. Usually only fearful thoughts would cause an attack. This JB had learned the hard way.

Finally everything that he would be shown on this visit had been shown, except the School of Knowledge. This he would experience tomorrow Earth time. For the rest of this day or space he would first have dinner with Whisper and then he would retire to his quarters for much needed re-energizing.

Wami escorted JB to the "Beauty of Planets Oceanraunt." This place was aptly named for never had JB experienced such splendor in a place to eat. A drink was placed in his hand as he stepped through the entrance. The taste was decidedly different and it was futile to try and guess at its contents. Wami waved the drink offering away as she would not be staying. The ceiling of the place was one massive dome which appeared to be of clear crystal. Beyond the dome all sorts of creatures from the sea swam overhead. It was like dining inside an aquarium without getting wet. The tables were draped with a metallic covering which gave the illusion of peace and JB was now starting to feel very cozy and comfortable from the effects of the drink. It was a mild aphrodisiac mixed in natural fruit juices made from plants of the sea, just enough to tease the senses, but not enough to create unnatural behavior. Sensual pleasure and good company was the intent and there was never such a thing as a hangover. The sea air which permeated the City would automatically cause the effects of the drink to dissipate as soon as one stepped from the oceanraunts, or social clubs.

JB glanced around the room again, his gaze settling on the blue flames rising from the center of each table. He blinked because it appeared that a goddess stepped from behind one of the flames. Shaking his head as if clearing it of some sort of fog, his eyes focused and locked on a pair of eyes he knew he'd never forget. Whisper walked toward him dressed in evening attire which would take every ounce of strength the man had, to remain the gentleman he knew he was expected to be. "Por Dios," his mind screamed. "Why do you torture me this way!" Hair swept up, Gems of ice-blue, Diamond Crystals coming from the center of her head to rest perfectly on the spot of the third eye, matching earrings and a pendant, which was connected to the top of her gown, exquisitely showed off her face and graceful swan neck. Shoulders and arms bare, the gown was gathered at the breast where the pendant connection met and cascaded like liquid water, in an iridescent waterfall, around the lower parts of her body. As she moved, the material would mold itself to the form underneath before seemingly dripping away.

JB began fighting a battle in his head. Someone spoke to him, he thought, but he didn't hear. Firecrackers were bursting, volcanoes were erupting, the Earth was cracking up right under his feet, but he felt absolutely wonderful.

"JB? JB are you alright?" Whisper was a little leery of the man standing before her. She'd not seen this look he was projecting during all of their travels together. At the same time the look caused excitement to rise within her and sensations she'd kept under control or thought she had put to rest back in the cave, came very near the surface.

She purposefully broke their locked gaze and turned to speak to Wami. "Thank You Wami." She hugged the other woman. "I give blessings to your departure and may your sleep be filled with the most beautiful dreams." Wami smiled and returned the positive energy she'd received. She turned, kissed JB's lips and extended protective blessings to him before departing.

Whisper turned once again to JB and smiling said, "Our table is over against the south wall. The Southern direction signifies the return of the Child within. A child trusts without judgment, loves unconditionally and their innocence allows them to enjoy life to the fullest. If treated with the same respect we as adults command, a child will be in your corner for the duration of a lifetime. What more could one ask for in the course of a relationship. She turned and re-traced the steps she'd taken to reach JB. From a rear view there was no gown from the small of her back, up. And Woman's naturalness, which Garth had spoken of during the swim to the city, re-entered JB's thoughts now. He knew he'd not forget this night, ever!

The two of them shared a wonderful closeness that evening and all too quickly the time passed. JB escorted Whisper to her quarters which were just around the corner from his own. She stood on her toes and kissed him gently and gave blessings. Unbelievably he was inwardly at peace. That night his dreams were blissful and it would have been fine with him if they never ended.

JB woke the next morning refreshed and anxious to begin the day. Garth appeared at his door and the monitor in his room switched on to show a grinning Garth asking permission to enter. JB thought, "of course, come in" and the doors opened before he had a chance to rise and attempt to open them. JB told Garth of what he was about to do and the two of them left JB's quarters talking and laughing like a couple of old friends. Which in truth, they really were.

CHAPTER 9
CLASS

The classroom JB found himself in was like no classroom he'd ever been in before. Here you actually lived the lessons so that once you walked back through those doors, you *"WOULD NOT"* forget anything that you learned. It was a Virtual Reality Learning Environment.

He learned that there was no such thing as Separation or Fragmentation of anything anywhere in the Universes. That included all planets, all entities, all animals, and all plants, everything that ever had been or ever would be created. That perceived rationale was myth, for **"ALL"** are **"ONE"**. **"EVERYTHING IS RELATED."** Other subjects included Parallel Realities, Dimensional Doorways, Reincarnation and many other Ancient Teachings that could only boggle the minds of the average person back on Earth. "No wonder there was no substance or structure to my Earth Life," JB thought to himself. "All the while I thought I was awake to the events going on around me, I was actually asleep!" This stuff was truly fascinating and JB found he had a thirst for more and more. The assignment which was given was to acquire the "Phoenix Journals" for an in-depth understanding. Before he knew it, class was at its end and not once had he gotten bored.

Once outside the door of the classroom, JB found Whisper waiting for him. She smiled and said, "Let's go to the gardens and have lunch."

Whisper and JB enjoyed a comfortable lunch. The gardens were unlike any JB had ever remembered seeing. Tropical plants and trees, with splashes of colors everywhere, made the comparison to 3rd Dimensional tropical gardens almost obsolete. Natural water routes cut through the garden lending a dream-like state to all who entered into its glory. Miniature bridges stretched across the waterways and disappeared through waterfalls, somewhat like the bridge and water-fall at the beginning of the journey, but on a smaller scale. Still, it over-rode the senses and made one instantly aware of how each and every facet of life was interwoven. Somehow the spirit blended with all the majestic images, causing one to lose oneself within the pictur-esque view stretched before them.

Whisper hesitated before breaking through the companionable si-lence she and JB shared. "It's time to show you something that I was not at liberty to present to you until now. Would you accompany me for one last excursion love? I think you will find this interesting if not down right exciting!"

She led the way across numerous bridges and finally entered a secret passageway behind one of the falls. Once within the passage-way, Whisper touched a rock on a ledge next to where they'd entered and the entrance was closed from view. She waved her hand through the air and the darkness flooded with a brilliant iridescent light.

"Why aren't we wet from walking through the falls?" JB asked. "Because," Whisper stated, "the water is only a simulation. Smells like water, refreshing, and feels like water, but actually it is only a product of the minds ability to recognize it for what it is meant to be. Quite simple really."

JB followed Whisper through a very narrow passageway to a platform slightly raised in a circular pattern at its end. There were three distinct markings on the surface of the platform floor. Whisper indicated that JB should stand on one of those markings as she took her place on another. A form began to take shape on the last mark-ing startling JB as he stood transfixed to the spot. He looked ques-tioningly at Whisper. She smiled and said, "JB, It pleases me to introduce to you one of the guides that have been with us from the very beginning of our journey. Please meet Dakkar of the Universal Galactic Fleet of Interstellar Travelers. He is High Counsel to the Order of the Ascended Galactic Tribunal Masters. He is number one of three." Whisper bowed slightly at the waist and addressed Dakkar. "Dakkar, I am proud to present to you, Jack Bonaparte Mitchell."

Dakkar caught and held JB's eye contact. Not quite sure what he should do, JB bowed slightly at the waist, taking Whisper's queue, and stated the name clearly and with deep respect and admiration. "Dakkar."

Dakkar responded with a humorous glitter within the eyes and never opening his mouth spoke to JB. "I am most honored to come face to face with one who holds such an exalted place among the souls of the chosen seven preordained for this particular mission at such an important time in the history of our vast Universe. Your life up until the time of your meeting Whisper at the Diner must have seemed of little significance. Yet, I say to you, every breath you breathed and every step you took, from babyhood up to this exact moment, was resided over and guided by those whose responsibility it was to bring you to where you now stand. Welcome Jack Bonaparte Mitchell.... JB."

To JB's surprise, Dakkar bowed slightly at the waist in return. Dakkar continued. "To your immediate left, there is an orange glowing orb. Wave your hand over it if you would, please." JB did as he was told and a pink warm fog began to swirl around his feet as a glass cylinder enclosed them on the platform. As the cylinder began to fill, JB was amazed at how far he'd come in developing the trust, that at one point in his life did not exist. When the fog had cleared, all three stood on a ledge which would be very hard to describe using words from the human language. Perhaps standing among the heavens would be a humble way of putting it. Before them, stretched as far as the eye could see, were myriads of stars and star clusters and heavenly gases so beautiful that it could take ones breath away.

JB thought his heart would explode from the sheer gloriousness of it all. The energy of love extended to him from each glittering mass slammed home to him just how little of the knowledge of love he actually knew. Would wonders never cease he thought? "No, Never," was Dakkar's reply. "Please follow, Whisper and JB."

Dakkar began rising as did Whisper. JB frowned, lifted a foot and ascended just as easily as the others. Placing both feet together, all three now walked on a seemingly invisible platform. Before them was a huge ship like nothing JB could have ever imagined.

Again, Dakkar's voice spoke to JB. "This is your anchoring dock within

this Galaxy and this is the 5th Dimensional gateway. There are others for other Soul groups on missions, though different, never the less just as important. Notice the emblem on your ship. One you should be quite familiar with by now." Dakkar smiled slightly. "When all seven of your Soul group have completed their inner quest of conquering unrest and have finally learned to let all things be solved and taken care of through faith and from within, as you and Whisper have JB, you will all receive orders from the Commander of the Universal Galactic Fleet of Interstellar Travelers. The most important of which will be teaching and sharing love unconditional throughout many Galaxies. We have watched each of you all of your lives and we know your hearts are of the kind needed to bring successful outcomes to all who you will encounter. We want you to be aware that your hearts are the kind of hearts which raise our vibratory beingness and exult us all. You are to be commended." Dakkar smiled the 1st brilliant smile since being introduced to JB. "So you see, JB, just how very important it is to have all seven of you here. Only then can this mission truly get under way. However, all things are on schedule." Smile gone, Dakkar states, "JB, I present this Ring of Galactic Royalty to you. Whisper couldn't tell you all before, but with this ring, you can never be harmed. It will become invisible to the naked eye once you return to the levels below this one, but it will always be with you. Only 'I' can remove it!"

JB looked at Whisper's finger and sure enough, there was her ring. She smiled at him rather sheepishly as though feeling slightly guilty at keeping this "Secret of Secrets" from him. Then she laughed that tinkling laugh JB had not heard since the 1st time on the golden stairway which had led to the platform on the sea.

Dakkar continued. "With this ring also comes a grave responsibility. The person you escort back to the 4th dimension has no such protection. You alone are their protection." Dakkar fixes JB with a stare so deep, JB shudders. "Do not worry. You have been guided and taught by the best, as has Whisper." Dakkar led the way back to the ledge. "Wave your hand JB."

JB complied and found himself spiraling through a tunnel at a speed unlike that of any speed he could compare it with during his life on the 3rd dimensional Earth. Whatever the vehicle he traveled upon, nothing could have prepared him for the sheer thrill he felt within himself as he landed beyond the double doors separating the 4th dimension from the 3rd. He was back at the bridge thinking of the paradoxical events which had taken place and of which he'd been a definite part.

Still on the 4th dimensional side of the bridge he became bathed in a beautiful light which shown softly as if through the mist and a voice speaks to him. It is neither male nor female.

"You have done us proud JB. You have anchored a place for yourself in the 4th dimension. But you have one more mission which must be completed before you claim your well deserved period of rest and reflection. Successfully, you grew spiritually enough to cross the bridge from the slumbering unenlightened world...to the unveiled, enlightened world of wakefulness. Now you must make one final entrance back into the third dimension to be of aide to the next semi-awake soul seeking its way along the mystical paths of truth. The next soul is awaiting you at an herb garden expo in the 3rd dimensional town called Joppatown. His name is Stephen Charles Winthrop. One of ageless wisdom. You will materialize as a gardener well versed in the knowledge of Herbal Medicinal Usage's, but you will avoid using a name just now. He is to be led to the wooden bridge just East of Joppatown in the forest. It crosses a deep ravine. You will remember. It is the place you were led to on your quest for truth. He will then make a decision on his own as to cross or not to cross the bridge. Many before him have turned away. Fear limits the growth of most people. Only those who are worthy will step beyond Earthly limitations........."

JB stood silently in awe as the voice faded and a quiet calm descended. Suddenly, he found himself magically transported back into the spiraling tunnel and opened his eyes to find that he and Whisper were back in the Gardens just beneath the waterfall where they had entered into the Secret passageway a few seconds ago. They walked back to their picnic spot and shared a dessert called Seaweed Pudding, a luscious tasting concoction filled with all sorts of natural vitamins and minerals. JB, concerned about his new instructions and the journey he was going to attempt, asked Whisper whether he would be late and was reminded that time here was not connected to "Earthly" third dimensional time.

Afterward they joined the Aqua people on the glass floor at the entrance to Mystic City. The Aqua people returned Whisper and JB to the platform in the sea. Once land legs had returned Whisper took JB's hand and led him up the steps to the circular bed at the top. "Lie down love." She handed him an apparatus which was very much like ear phones. She sat on the side of the bed, holding his hands. "This last stretch of the journey you must travel alone. When you get to the big doors, you will know you've reached the boundaries of the fourth dimension. When you awaken, you will find that you have retraced our steps and will find yourself at your appointed destination. It will be your mission now to guide he who crosses the bridge here to the fourth dimension entrance. You will remember everything, you will forget nothing, and you will teach well." She reached down and kissed him. "I will be here when you return. Now close your eyes" ....and Whisper and the aqua people were gone.

JB opened his eyes and after a second of confusion, recognized the place where he was lying was not on the platform, but on a soft bed of mulch behind a row of evergreens. After pausing for a moment and wondering if that waitress had drugged him, he arose, checked to see that he was wearing clothes and walked around the corner of the row of trees. He was indeed in a garden center and there were people milling around looking at plants on display. As he stood there confused, a man walked over and said, "Excuse me, isn't all this great? Do you know about herbs? My name is Stephen Winthrop and I am looking for the rare local herb selection."

JB paused for only a second before replying, remembering instructions to not give his name just now, so he said instead, "Hi! If you want to see a spot where some really magical herbs grow, forget this show and go for a little ride with me to a place I know near a stream. I can answer some of your questions and believe me, you will never regret it…….."

INTERIM

THE JOURNEY

All 7 of the chosen souls grew enough, spiritually, to reach the Fourth Dimensional realms. They had incarnated to the 3rd dimensional realms to help raise the spiritual vibrations of the humans who inhabited the Earth. Each had been born through human channels with no conscious memory of who they truly were. Each had no memory of their previous existences as higher vibration beings. They had lived their mortal lives as any other human might.

With the struggle to conquer unrest and build and hold tight to the faith of the ONE Universal Creator, their individual missions had been accomplished with great success. Now as all 7 stood before Dakkar on the landing pod, rings of Galactic commendation now on everyone's middle finger of the right hand, gleaming as brilliantly as the star clusters that surrounded them, Dakkar decreed that each were from this moment forward ordained as the 2nd highest ranking commanding officers within the Universal Galactic Star Fleet of the Pleadian Interstellar Travelers. With this honor also came the returned, here to fore veiled, memory of who each of them truly were.

Whisper was in actuality Janara. Everyone in the Pleadian Sector called her Jana. She was also the beloved Daughter of Dakkar. She was brilliant beyond her years and no one would even bother to *try* to match wits with her except Ashzar. Dakkar had bestowed an even higher rank upon JB, known in the Pleiades as Ashzar. He was dubbed High Commander of *ALL* the Pleiadian Star Fleets and was topped only by the Superior Counsel of Commanders of the Universal Galactic Star Fleet of the Pleiadian Interstellar Travelers. Ashzar was chosen, thus, due not only to his unique strategical mind, but also because of his ability to place himself within the emotional molecular structures of others which gave him the advantage of solving most difficult situations while leaving ones dignity intact. His diplomacy was unequalled. Stephen was known as Konvaser (pronounced Con vay' zer) and was among one of the highest honored Commanders in the Pleadian Sector as well as sectors throughout many Universes. His advice was sought from many Galaxies in the Universe as his medicinal expertise rivaled that of no other.

And so on with the other 4 chosen souls whose main ongoing mission was that of Earth. In addition to their Earth assignment, each with their own specialties would be assigned to separate individual missions once they'd had time to rest in their natural home environment. Each, that is, except Jana who always seemed to end up on dual missions with Ashzar. There was a conspiracy going on between Dakkar and Ashzar – of this Jana was certain. But, try as she might she couldn't seem to make her father understand that she didn't need to be protected. Especially when ASHZAR was her protector!

Ashzar knew that Jana became irritated each time a new mission was assigned to him. He knew that Jana would always be assigned to that mission also due to an oath he'd given her father many ions before. Dakkar looked upon Ashzar as the Son he'd never had, so it was only natural that he'd want his son to look out for his only daughter. Every once in a while Ashzar would use these opportunities just to rile Jana. He loved to see the fire in her eyes and she exhilarated his blood because, as he saw it, she belonged to him. He admired the wildness that he knew could never be tamed and he'd have it no other way. So he decided to pen her a short Poem. If only he could see her face

when she received it by way of courier.

My Dearest Jana –
There once was a daughter of Decker
Whose face was so cute you could peck her
But when she got mad, and wrote to her dad
He sent Ashzar over to check her.
>>>
There'll be a new mission within minutes
And believe me my dear you'll be in it
So spare me the tears and get on over here
For the sooner you arrive….we can begin it.
Love, Ashzar

• •

Jana definitely was not amused, she was thoroughly confused
As to why her father liked Ashzar for any reason.
From the time she was born, Ash had been a constant thorn
And her father's part in these episodes bordered on treason.
>>>
There must be a way, to make Ashzar pay
For all the frustrations he'd caused Jana yearly.
And whatever the price, it would not be too nice
For she'd always dreamed of crushing Ashzar most dearly.
>>>
Whatever she'd say, Ash always got in the way
And her temperament was not that of a Lady's.
Then a thought crossed her mind, in the swiftest record of time
Why not – constant missions for Ash away from the Pleiades.
>>>
Jana approached her Dad, and she was not at all sad
For she knew Dakkar would approve this assignment.
There was unrest in the Stars, and especially Mars
T'would require Ash's expertise in reconstructive Time Align-
ment.
>>>
But what Jana didn't know, was what Dakkar didn't show

That he knew without Ashzar around, Jana would be trouble.
So the assignment he approved and he "would not" be moved
When he decreed Jana would accompany Ash as his double.
>>>
Jana snatched the signed page, as she flew in a rage
And hurled space words at Dakkar we won't mention.
She could not believe, how Dakkar could deceive
His own daughter "knowing" she was consumed by this tension.
>>>
Dakkar ignored Jana's plea, for he'd raised her you see
And he thought it best her warring emotions for Ash be put aside.
But Jana would not give in, at all cost she would win
For you see, for Jana, this had cut deeply her pride.
>>>
Jana turned on her heel, seething with anger still
And on her way out of Dakkar's chambers, ran smack into Ashzar.
There was a twinkle in his eye and he knew she would try
To undo the orders – so smiling said…."meet me later at the Bar."
>>>
Uncontrollable rage (forget grace), Her hand snaked across his face
To bring the insoluble grin to a halt.
She stepped back at the glare, rebounding from his stare
And thought, "I forgot my laser. Damn!! It's locked in the vault!
>>>
Not pushing her luck, with the man she'd just struck!
Jana backed very cautiously out of harms way.
Ashzar grinned like a prince, which made Jana wince
Then to Ash, swore, "On my honor – Father's Pet- you will pay!"
>>>
Her next actions she didn't trust, so leave she must
And stamping her foot, turned toward the Universal Escalator.

Ashzar stopped her retreat, as he lifted her off her feet
Face close to hers whispered, "Later Jana, 'I WILL' see you later."
>>>
Knees up quick as a flash, she pushed away from Ash
And eyes glaring she mouthed a murderous statement.
She turned on her heel, tears threatening to spill
Space definitely was needed to achieve anger abatement.
>>>
Ashzar watched her depart, but there was joy in his heart
As he silently thanked Dakkar's strategic command.
For he knew deep within, his intent was to win
And in this Jana had no grounds on which to stand.
>>>
The struggle was rough, but Jana stood tough
For the power of the two men was much more than a mighty thrust.
But Jana was no wimp – OH NO! rather quite the mischievous imp
And they realized her power, alone, was one not to trust.
>>>
Thinking deeply in thought, of the battle she'd just fought
Trying to "RAZZ" the brute Ashzar to hate her -
An idea came to her then, with no other goal but to win
She'd elicit help from a friend called Drake Traitor!
>>>
Now Drake Traitor by far, couldn't stomach Ashzar
And his feelings for Jana could be compared to melted butter.
With her mind running free, and happily laughing with glee
She'd pit Drake and Ashzar one against the other.
>>>
Jana put through a fax and sat back to relax
For she'd changed her name on the decree to Drake Traitor.
Ash would find she'd been pulled and he'd rage like a bull
Laughing aloud Jana said, "Right again Ash, Be seeing 'ya Later!"

Pleiadian Galactic Decree

Let it be known on this millisecond of Pleiadian existence that Ashzar of the Pleiades is forthwith assigned to first – Mars and is to deal with the abominable unrest of that sector of the Galaxy and second – Earth, to assist the souls there who are reaching for spiritual guidance from these realms on which we abide.
>>>
Let it also be known that Drake Traitor will accompany Ashzar as his double taking all direction from the High Commander of the Galactic Star Fleet.
>>>
Let it also be known that what this counsel has so decreed – let no sentient creature tamper with the contents herein.

Superior Counsel of Commanders of the
Universal Galactic Star Fleet
Of Interstellar Travelers

Jana knew that a copy of the altered Decree would be sent to Ashzar, but she gambled on the fact that as busy as Ash stayed, he might just miss the alteration. Too bad....Ash would handle the disappointment. Ash always knew how to handle difficult things. She smiled to herself feeling quite elated.

CHAPTER 10
MINOR BUSINESS

Ashzar was greatly amused by the little game Jana had going on him. He understood that she had good reason to be jealous and harbor ill feelings toward him. He sat in his quarters on the command ship and decided that since it was a harmless episode, perhaps he should play along for a while and see if maybe Dakkar's daughter could learn something from the exchange and grow a little in the process. He loved her dearly and had made a solemn oath to Dakkar to protect her, but that did not mean shielding her from the realities of the real Universe. On the other hand, it certainly was invigorating to have a challenge from a worthy opponent. He was really getting tired of babysitting this solar system.

Dakkar and Ashzar were both aware that Jana would be a being that the Universe was privileged to see only occasionally in its history. Of course, Dakkar was allowed to be slightly prejudiced because it was his daughter. Ashtar simply assumed it would be so because it was his old friend's daughter and genetics mean a lot. Early in her childhood, Jana seemed destined to become somewhat of a challenge to Ashzar. He assumed at her birth that he would get to play the kindly uncle to her, but it just never seemed to work out along those lines. She was smart beyond her physical years. She was prone to playing games that would make those Earthlings down there see her as a goddess (they had those perceptions you see) in any earlier age.

Ashzar smiled to himself as he remembered her antics during the

Armachron II uprisings. Sure, the results had been the reversal of a military situation that could have destroyed a star, but in his mind, youngsters were supposed to heed the warnings from their elders and leave external affairs of other races alone. The fact that every visitor arriving at the main transporter pod on Armachron II passed by a larger than life 3D Hologram display of her was testimony to the fact that diplomacy came about in strange and wondrous ways sometimes. Ashzar was reminded to stop in and visit Ambassador Ohmigosh if he ever passed that way again.

A message from communications jerked Ashzar back to reality. He was reminded of the responsibility he had here in this system and decided he had better get back to his duties. Still, the Daughter of Dakkar was a pleasant visage in his mind and he hastily drafted a response to her poem of nearly Epic Proportions that she had written even though it had been sent, in error, along by courier with the Decree Assignment. Ashzar Penned........

"Jana, Daughter of Duckeur, please be advised through this communications that there are certain restrictions and responsibilities that everyone under that umbrella of this joint command must follow, to wit:

>> Universal Code of Justice, Species 19, Subsection 37, as recorded in the Akashic Records. Standard 425, subparagraph 97HD clearly states that "All sentient beings, given to clearly understand the basic concepts of The Law be expressly forbidden to send any form of Trans-space communication under false identification." <<

"I am sure it comes as no surprise to you that while it seems I spend the majority of my time communicating with humans trying to save themselves, my staff always stands ready to inform me of any improprieties within the structure of this Command. Therefore, in the game afoot, I call a foul and must issue this warning. No harm done, certainly, but just like the mythical Santa Claus, I am watching you. Rest assured that you are still stuck here, I am still Commander Ashzar and we can proceed in a civil manner from this point forward. Join me for dinner this evening if you dare. Cordially, Ash."He hated to tip his hand about surveillance techniques in the fleet, but rules were meant to be challenged, not broken.

Jana knew JB would do all he could to overturn the final papers sent in to the Tribunal. So Jana decided to meet him at the bar, even though she knew he didn't really expect her, simply because he went there at a certain time every night. Ashzar was not the type to over-indulge, but tonight would be special. He was leaving on a mission and he and his comrades would be toasting farewells. Just to make sure Ash didn't find out about the change in plans before he went to his ship, Jana thought she'd just play along with things, the way that Ash thought they really were.

Jana met Ash as he stepped through the door of the Social Club. "Hi Ash. Thought I'd be a good sport about things since we have a very long job to do ahead of us. Here. I know what your favorite drink is, so this one is on me." Jana had two drinks, space juice, in her hand and she knew the one she handed Ash he'd insist she drink from first. So she handed him hers and when he gave it back and told her to take a sip, eyes glittering in that dangerous way of his, Jana acted hurt and said, "Damn, Ash. I'd have thought you trusted me better than that by now. But to show you I mean you no harm, take mine and I'll drink this one." She switched Drinks with him and Ash downed the cooling liquid. He teasingly asked for a kiss and Jana said, "Dance with me first and I'll think about your request after that." Ashzar laughed aloud and said, "May I have this dance?"

Before the 1st quarter of the song was over, Ashzar stumbled and things started going blurry before his eyes. When he finally under-stood what was happening, he made one last attempt to go for Jana's throat. Laughing, Jana snapped her fingers and a muscular couple of friends came over to retrieve Ashzar. "Take him directly to his ship. This stuff will wear off in a couple of hours and by then it'll be to late for Ashzar to do anything about pulling strings to capture me," she stated smiling. "I'll take care of all the necessary paperwork he'd have been responsible for and no one will be the wiser. Thanks Guys. I owe you one."

After some time had passed, Ashzar could hear a strange sound off in the distance. It was the sound of water flowing or…. OUCH! His head seemed to explode with a deep-seated pain that was burst-ing out of nowhere. He sat up, opened his eyes and found that he was in his own quarters. Slowly, memories of his meeting with Jana in the Social Club before dinner came seeping like a ground fog into his mind. "Flagensturr!" he swore. Jana had done it to him again. That little song and dance routine with the space juice had turned out the way things usually did and she had beaten him again.

Despite the ebbing pain in his head, he smiled to himself and forgave her. He knew she meant no harm when she played the role of free spirit. Her heart was filled with love and her spirit was alive and vital. She simply hated to be told what to do and refused to accept that he was in charge. It was plain that he had made the wrong choice to play the role of Uncle to this Daughter of Dakkar.

As the pain left completely, he smiled again and at the same time groaned inwardly. By now the security team, responsible for making sure she was aboard ship for the mission back to Earth, should have her securely locked away in her cabin. He felt it necessary to arrange this little surprise after her threats to not accompany him, even though she knew her father's wishes all too well. At least he should have been spared the headache. Ashzar smiled to himself yet again and reminded himself that he would have to talk to Dakkar about giving him a bonus for taking her out of his realm for an, as yet, undetermined period of time.

If only those stubborn humans on Earth would wake up and see the God in themselves, see the destruction they were bringing to their beautiful green planet, learn again to love, he could get on to other missions. The Universe was anxiously awaiting the end of this latest chapter of human evolution. The time was near and Ashzar felt the burden of responsibility wearing heavy as he made his way to the bridge to get underway. Jana would be mad, but she was so beautiful when she was mad and somehow, Ashzar could not get the thought of spending a year or so in Earth orbit with her to leave his mind. She was special and he knew destiny was not through with the two of them.

Jana had expected Ash to take precautions just in case she got out of hand. Ash was Brilliant! She hand no choice but to concede that. She was way above average in intelligence, but Ash was just down right Brilliant and this always made her work extra hard to outwit him. This time was no different. She knew in her heart he'd do everything within his power (and powerful he was) to make sure she was with him on this trip. There was nothing he wouldn't and couldn't do because he had her father's full backing. This was where the restless feelings came in. On Earth these types of feelings would be taken to a whole other level to the extent that the term used would be

"Jealousy." There was no tolerance in these realms for those types of emotions and if one should happen to convey such emotions, steps would be taken to immediately rectify those stirrings because they would surely lead to destruction. Jana knew her father loved her with all his heart, but Ash was the son He'd always wanted. So in his mind Jana and Ash are a pair and he'd have it no other way. Not that the final decision wouldn't swing in that direction if Jana were allowed to decide on her own. Dakkar, however, wasn't leaving anything to chance and Ashzar loved her enough, she knew, to protect her with his very last breath. Wonderful Guy, but no one would force her to do anything she didn't want to do. She'd give them hell until she was ready to do otherwise. In the meantime – let Ash worry over her well being, she thought laughing. She intended to live as dangerously as the Universe would allow.

Jana had reasoned that Ash would know were her mind might lead her. Ash always had this uncanny way of knowing what she might do before Jana did, but not this time. She would outwit him this time. In her boot was a Stun tube – no bigger than her little finger and flat as a piece of paper. This little piece of equipment could not wage a war, but could buy approximately 30 minutes of life saving time should you find yourself hemmed up with an enemy. Jana knew Ash would, as a precaution, have her watched and bodily taken to his ship if it became necessary. She knew that his crew followed his every order and would not fail him if it were at all within their power. Well – Jana intended to UN-empower them if it came to that. They'd be fine, Ash would understand. After seeing Ashzar take a nose dive behind Jana's machinations, they'd know to put whatever plan Ash had set into place, in action. So when the two 7 foot guards approached her with this amused look on their faces, Jana didn't even put up a struggle. She simply said, "I've been expecting you," and flashed them a brilliant smile.

Jana watched as Ashzar was being carried out the door of the Social Club, but smiled as she was escorted out some short distance behind him. As she suspected, she was led to Ashzar's ship and into quarters he'd instructed she be taken to. Jana quickly surveyed her surroundings and after being asked if anything could be gotten for her to make her more comfortable, Jana replied no, but she requested that the guards shift some of the furniture in the room to positions more to her liking. The guards closed and locked the door just as a precautionary measure which made Jana smile even more. "Morons" she thought, almost not containing the feelings of euphoria she was beginning to feel. Adrenaline pumping through her veins, Jana had to focus on the mission at hand.

Not paying attention now, comfortable that Jana couldn't leave the room, the guards bent to hoist chairs and other furniture as Jana instructed them. She joked and laughed with them as though they were old buddies of hers. They really were, but their allegiance was to Ashzar first. Retrieving her stun tube from her boot, she casually walked up to each man and gently touched the arm on each one. The energy from the tube was powerful enough to penetrate even armor and both slumped to the floor. "Sorry guys," she thought. "This has nothing to do with either of you. It's just that you've gotten in the way."

Quickly she bends down to take the spectra from the dark haired one's space belt. She opens the door and cautiously steps out into the hall. Knowing that Ash would leave no stones unturned, she found a hidden tunnel way just beyond her door. She removed the grate there and crawled in. Cramped spaces, but Jana knew this ship inside out. She'd made it her business because she knew that knowledge would someday be to her advantage. Crawling on her belly and moving more quickly than the average light body, she soon landed outside the ship and onto the floor just above another grate leading under the landing pad. Undoing the grate was no small feat, but, Jana had been a pro at removing these things since childhood. Once inside, she slid the lid back into place and climbed the short ladder to the underground tunnel. Feet on the floor, Jana tore into a run knowing time was ticking quickly against her.

She rounded a corner and came up against a situation she'd not counted on. "Damn!!!" she thought. "Damn you, Ashzar." Ducking back behind a corner insert, she desperately commanded herself to quiet her breathing. "Think, Jana. Think!" she admonished herself. Two guards were standing by the entry way to the tunnel she needed to get through. There were two other tunnels in the same vicinity and those were blocked too!

Against the opposite side of the tunnels was a storage area filled with debris waiting to be transported out of the docking area. Jana took a safety flare from her belt, pulled the cap, and tossed it into the storage space. It caught and the contents burst into flames. Chaos broke loose and guards scurried to put out the flames. In the interim of all the confusion, Jana made her break and literally flew down the tunnel to the short stairs to another grate which led back up to the landing pod, but on a different side. Another ship awaited her there.

CHAPTER 11
SPACE CHASE

J ana took three steps at a time into the ship designed especially to her specifications. It was sleek and fast. Outfitted to ward off the mightiest of attacks and made to take on the effect of invisibility if necessary, but invisibility only lasted a specified amount of time before the systems could recharge to become invisible once again. When this happened it took an expert mind to be able to keep the advantage. Jana hadn't been outwitted yet!

Not wasting any time, Jana ran down the Daily log check list. "All hands aboard? Supplies as instructed? All Systems go? Engage the Engines! Build power thrust to one third accommodations! Ease her out of the docking bay!" Seconds ticked by. "Is she clear of the docking pad?" Jana hesitates to give time for the ship to move ahead. "Enough distance from the station for full power? Wonderful! Full thrust ahead, ladies, Run like hell!"

Jana checks her wrist meter. Ashzar should be coming out of his imprisonment in about 5 minutes. Once his orientation was brought back to where he could move, another 5 minutes should have passed. Time was crucial and she smiled imagining his anger. She wouldn't want to be a part of his crew when he awakened. By the time he'd figured out what was afoot, she'd be long gone to a destination she'd been careful to keep to herself. The crew manning her ship was all Women. Top female officers; all with a reason for competing with the males of the planet. One female had volunteered to help Jana with her mission, but Jana was on to that one. Jana knew she had a soft side for Ashzar and though Jana was not of the mind to give in to Ashzar, she didn't necessarily want anyone else getting his attentions either. This female could not be trusted, so she was purposely given erroneous instructions to ensure all information she might feed back to Ash would be false.

Jana sat down and her mind wandered back to the time of the Armachron II uprisings. Ashzar had been adamant about her staying out of external affairs because children (she had been a teenager), had no knowledge of the goings on of Universal problems. But Jana was constantly around Dakkar and Ashzar and she knew much more than she was given credit for. She'd proved that to them, the hard way of course. She also remembered how Ash had saved her butt from two Ambassadors who were determined to spirit her away with them. Thank goodness to him for that! Her females' wiles had only worked against her where those two were concerned. Somehow she'd gotten in their life-force systems and only Ash was smart enough to untangle her from that mess. She smiled remembering how he'd ranted and raved at her. She'd said, "Oh Ash, I wanted you to feel important too! I purposely set things up that way so you could come to my rescue." Then she'd given him this big hug and walked away knowing she'd thanked the stars over and over again for sending him in just the nick of time.

Her mind back to the moment, she checked her time meter again. Ash's ship was huge. It moved at a pretty good clip but she'd gotten way ahead of him and she had some plans that should throw him off her trail. She knew he'd abort the mission to Earth and come for her. His anger would demand it. And.....Dakkar would agree to his reasoning for delaying such an important project. Boy....she'd think about the possibility of never being able to return home again later on. Right now.....there was adventure ahead of her and for now, that was enough.

Ashzar could still feel the effects of whatever Jana had slipped into his drink. He gathered his wits and started off toward the command center to ascertain that the ship was fully prepared for the journey ahead. He actually found himself humming a little tune as he thought about the way Jana's plan to escape had backfired and again a smile crossed his face. He would have to work hard to appear seriously angry with her when he had her brought to his cabin later.

Arriving at the command center, Ashzar was pleased to see that everything was in order and that the crew was doing the usual fine job of running the ship. The navigator had a minor technical problem with the mind-master computer link, but it was soon corrected and all looked ready for the journey to begin. He ordered her to take the ship into a holding orbit and await further orders.

Ashzar sat silently watching the view-screen as the spaceport receded from view. It was no different from watching a holosaga or news broadcast. There was no feeling of motion as the inertia generators compensated for all accelerations experienced by the massive space craft. Many thoughts of the upcoming mission crossed his mind as he made mental contact with some of the humans on earth. Channeling might be all the rage there, but to Ashzar it was a sacred duty to contact those who reached the developmental stage necessary to allow direct one on one contact. His mind was relaxed so the various duties it was being called upon to perform could all happen simultaneously. His primary focus was on getting the ship into clear space for acceleration into multi-dimensional space, but other activities went on at the same time and he called each of them to the forefront of his thought periodically to monitor them.

Finally, Ashzar decided to give a call to his companions and see how mad Jana was after the way he'd ordered her brought aboard the ship. He mentally sent out a signal and waited for their replies. Ashzar was still monitoring the departure sequence when the alarm bells started a mild ringing in his head. Surely Jana's guards were awake, but when he focused a bit more of his concentration on them, there was simply no thought patterns coming through at all. Suddenly, Ashzar knew that he would not be hearing the repost he anticipated from his guards. He rose swiftly and with a nod to his first officer to proceed with departure, he headed for his quarters. Even away from the noisy command center, Ashzar was surprised at the relative quiet in the mental bands. He focused a little more of his attention on their thought patterns and still only received white noise. Now those alarm bells were screaming at him!

At his quarters, a quick scan of the computer showed that Jana and her bodyguards came aboard as expected, but he could not locate them. Additional scans of the records told him in milliseconds that they were still in her private quarters, but that she was no longer aboard ship. He rechecked the records and in less than a second, was convinced that she had figured a way to overpower the guards and leave the ship without a trace. Momentary confusion crossed his brow as he attempted to pick up her trail out of the ship. Dang that child! If he did not love her so much and owe such allegiance to her father, he would refuse these babysitting missions altogether. It was, however, a way to spend time with her and observe as she grew into the companion he someday hoped would consent to be his partner. Reality asserted itself abruptly as the com-link beeped and the command center asked permission to enter hyperspace. Ashzar quickly sent a burst message to the navigator asking her to hold position until he could solve a minor personal problem. He could not leave for Earth without locating Jana and assuring her safety. He asked his security chief to meet him in his cabin and began to formulate new curses to heap upon Jana's head when he found her.

While Ashzar made it his business to track Jana, Jana was intent on making sure Ash never found her, but if it had to be that way, she'd sure make him sweat and admit to the fact that she could be a worthy opponent to anyone, that she could stand right along side him with the best. She'd make him say those words or be permanently separated from this dimensional realm trying.

To her second in command, Jana said, "Tell Marina to check the density of the mass before us. We need to sit the ship down and disengage all instruments for a time. Ashzar and his crew are great trackers, but they need viable energy in order to do that. Ashe's mind-master computer link is futuristically way ahead of any in the Universe. We need to simply disappear for an hour or two." That would mean going into a mental comatose state and Jana had trained everyone here to do just that. She had practiced shutting down her mind since she was very young. These were the times Ash became confused. He could not get a fix on her location until she forgot and relaxed those brain cells in her mind. Over the years she'd gotten really good with a total shutdown for long periods of time. She knew it frustrated Ashzar because he had no clue of what she did from time to time. He prided himself on knowing the moves of everyone on their planet when he wanted to tune in. Jana was the exception and probably the reason he sometimes drank more space juice than he was accustomed to. Call her a child. How old must she be before he looked upon her as a woman? He truly needed to get over the "Uncle" crap. Jana grinned. It was simply his way of putting her in her place. It would work momentarily and then Jana would make him pay in ways she knew would irritate him. So, if it was a child he wanted, a child she would be. But oh! The man did not know what he was missing! Jana laughed aloud at her own sense of humor.

Mind back to the present, Jana stared out the huge monitor like viewer on the bridge. The mass ahead, perhaps a solfatara star, had mistiness about it now, as if fluid had gathered over the ionized orb, vanishing, then returning; like a heart beating. The light of the galaxy was refracting, as if folding into itself. Jana stared into the dark matter mist, hunting for the structure she'd seen only moments ago. She spoke as if making a statement to herself, "It isn't stable ....is it Marina."

"No Commander," Marina answered. "The density registers as plasmatic decay. Its density is much too high, an inferno of sorts. I would not recommend trying to sit the ship on its surface. Factually, I would suggest getting as far away from the mass, as quickly as possible."

Jana saw the wisdom in the advice of her first in Command. "#1, Reverse Thrusters. Change course to a southeast temporary charting position. Let's see what this mystery before us unfolds." The crew moved the ship to a safer distance and placed her in auto mode. Everyone on the bridge moved closer to the view monitor watching the display before them. The surface of the star was almost molten now. It was subsiding, collapsing inward, but not like any star Jana had ever seen about to self destruct. This was different. The projections of the star's formation, based on Pleiadian mathematics, did not add up to what had been taught to her by Ashzar. It looked like a kaleidoscope, colors intertwining and merging in and out like a ball of vapor. This was a bomb planted here for some unsuspecting visitor. Why? Jana had no clue, but she was sure they'd soon find out.

Snapping out of her trance like state – Jana yelled...."Turn her about. Engage all extra booster power! This baby is about to go!" Jana didn't need to issue those commands. Everyone was already heading for their stations. Odd was not the word to describe the transformation of the "thing" in front of them. It pulsated, it breathed, it seemed full and menacing and at that exact moment she made the atomic bomb seem like an infant as she ripped apart like nothing ever heard of in Pleiadian History. The impact upon the ship from the force of the blast threw Jana & her crew around the bridge like so many rag dolls.

A gale blew the ship on a course, no one there would ever have dreamed of attempting. Fortunately no one was seriously hurt. All hands waived medical attention. "Lucky for us we weren't any closer. The debris from the blast alone would have cut us to ribbons. #2 send someone below to assess the damage. Lieutenant Bry, what systems are down and how soon can we bring them back on-line." The lieutenant answered Jana. "Damn, that long," Jana whistled thru her teeth. "Alright. Let's do what has to be done to get this baby in top shape. How are the shields holding? Hopefully, we won't need them, but it's nice to know the shape we're in just in case of an at-tack."

"Shields are two quarters operational sir."

"Wonderful," Jana said in almost a whisper. The wheels in her mind were beginning to turn. A thought popped into her head and she wondered how she could have forgotten to ask sooner. "Lieuten-ant, what about the manual backup systems? Can we use those until the computerized systems are on-line?" The lieutenant checked out the manual system which seemed in working order. Reporting to Jana she said, "There is only one problem commander." "Speak up lieutenant," was Jana's reply. "Sir, a beam has fallen across the main Turbo Shoots to the ship's manual Expulsion lines. If we can't peri-odically change patterns on the winged flaps, steering this baby may be next to impossible.

Jana smiled. "Lieutenant where is your faith in Woman Power?" Aloud she commanded, "All hands listen up. We need to pool our strength to clear the turbo lines. Let's get it done. We're sitting ducks here." I won't give Commander Ashzar the satisfaction of seeing us crippled. He'd dearly love that, Jana thought.

In no time the Turbo lines were clear. Cheers went up from the crew. The ship cruised at a steady pace until the main systems were back up and running. Manual motivation was discontinued and the ship picked up speed. "Commander! We are not in familiar terri-tory. To be blunt – I've no clue as to where we are. The gale blew us through a strange black hole, that much registered on our systems and one other thing sir......" the navigator coughed, "we are not moving under our own power. We're being pulled by some unknown force."

Jana paled. "No need for panic. We'll ride this out and see were it leads us. Until then everyone relax as much as possible. Save your strength and ideas for later." To herself she thought, "Something tells me we're going to need all the stamina we can muster." She had wanted to escape mind link communications with Ash, but she hadn't entertained thoughts of doing it this way. Damn! Damn! Damn! What had she gotten herself into this time?

Ashzar surveyed his command ship and convinced that all was in order, proceeded to locate Jana. He stilled his mind and sought her energy among the universe. He was well aware that she could shut herself off from him for brief periods, but he was counting on her being busy with the escape and using at least a portion of her mind. Suddenly, a tidal wave of mind-energy burst in his head like a sudden bright light in the darkness. He quickly withdrew his search and scanned his ship's systems. All seemed in order locally, so he spread his awareness outward seeking the source of the blast. As his awareness chased the pulse of the energy across light-years, he began to sense the faintest trace of something familiar. Like a flash of color in a raging torrent, he sensed the smallest bit of energy within the massive wave spreading across several dimensions. Jana! It had to be her. Recognition of her subtle energy within the massive storm of energy was both startling and scary.

Ashzar could not imagine that she had been the cause of such a catastrophe. Such strange energies as were in this force were unknown to him. He quickly scanned the ships sensors and could glean no usable data to explain the rip in the usual flow and surge of the Universes. His mind raced to make some sense of the trace of Jana riding on this wave. Could she have been killed by the cause of the new energies? Was she sending a distress signal to him?

Ashzar was not accustomed to not knowing. He quickly surveyed key personnel on the command ship as well as powerful contacts throughout the Universe. No answers were forthcoming. No being, within his knowledge, could offer any explanation to the energy burst or Jana's presence within it. He summoned his staff to an instant mind-melding and sought the next course of action. When he spoke, the Universe reverberated with the power of his energy. "My niece Jana may be involved somehow with that massive disturbance in the Universal Energy some of you just experienced. The mission to Earth is suspended until we locate the source of the explosion and Locate Jana."

Immediately, the Positronics Officer, Narborivck, joined in, "Commander, the source of the energy disturbance lies about 2 light years distance in the vicinity of a previously explored Solfatara type star in the Gamma 17 quadrant."

Ashzar knew exactly which Solfatara star Narborivck was describing. He could not for a microsecond imagine that Jana would or could be anywhere near the quadrant, but he was prepared to listen to any explanation for the past moment's strange events. Easing his mind deeper into its highest state, he again scanned space and time for Jana. Nothing! Absolutely nothing! Either the life-force that was Jana had been totally annihilated or there was something shielding her energy. He must know!

Throwing conventional wisdom to the winds, Ashzar asked the Creator for strength and ordered his massive Command Ship to the location of the Solfatara star. Micro-seconds seemed like hours as his crew linked minds with the ship's systems and headed across space at speeds that would have driven A. Einstein mad could he have conceived of them. As he mentally scanned the region of space where he was headed, Ashzar noted several small black holes in the vicinity as well as one cluster of anti-matter. Nothing made sense anymore. The solfatara star was no more; no debris field was evident, no stray light-speed particles coming toward him. Nothing. Not even the very faint trace of Jana's energy was evident any longer. It was as if something was sucking every known band of energy in the region away to some undetectable place. For the first time in many seasons, Ashzar began to experience fear.

CHAPTER 12
NEW FRONTIER

J ana turned over the running of her ship to her 1st in Command. She needed the solitude of her own Quarters. Once there – the first thing she did was to scan the computers to see if anything had been overlooked around the powerlessness of being in control of her own ship. She creased her brow and thought how strange this all was. Someone had been watching them and waiting. The more she thought about it, the surer she was about it because the Solfatara star did not explode until she was safely out of harms way. Whoever was behind all this knew she was smart enough to distance herself once the Volcanic like activity began to pick up pace. Funny, when she'd first thought of putting her ship down on its surface, there was no activity at all. Someone had locked onto her ships systems even back then and had probably known she intended to land. That was the exact moment the mists began to cover the star. But.......why!

Scanning the systems again, Jana saw that the systems seemed to be functional, but something was not quite right. The circuit gauges weren't fluctuating on the viewer scales as they should be. The Amplitude Modulation System and the Frequency Modulation Bands were showing varying degrees of Orange running up and down the monitors instead of Red. That could only mean one thing! Another ship had overridden the capabilities of Jana's ship. And it also meant that they had locked on to her energy grids to tow her along. It ALSO MEANT the ship responsible for this must be *INVISIBLE*. Of Course!

Jana sat down to calm her breathing which had become agitated in the course of her Brain Storming session. Perhaps it was time to give up the stubbornness and at least get a connection line to Ashzar in case this situation turned ugly. She mentally slowed down her pulse rate and breathed deeply…in and out…formulating a rhythm that was powerful enough to take her out of body. She envisioned herself inside Ashzar's ship on the bridge. She opened her eyes and saw Ashzar sitting with a frown across his brow. How she loved this man. She walked up to him and reached out her hand. "Ashzar." Ashzar looked up and there was a puzzled look on his face which seemed to change to resigned defeat. Jana continued to speak. "I'm in the wormhole near the Southeast side of the Gamma 17 Quadrant. The Solfatara star was there. It's no more." She pointed to his computerized scanner and showed him the wormholes as she was speaking. Jana hesitated and wondered what was wrong. Ash should know to tune in. He should be able to hear her and she him, but she couldn't feel him and this had never happened before.

Jana was becoming alarmed and her vision began fading in and out. She was having immense trouble holding the energy which kept her out of body. Something was causing her to pull back. She pointed out the worm hole once again on his systems. The same one her systems had shown her ship had been pulled into. She cupped her hands in a circle and moved her hands around 3 times to indicate three – 360 degree turns. She pointed to Ashzar's ship, then the wormhole and moved her hands in rapid succession around, and around, and around. It was all she could do. Her energy was sapped and she was back in her body.

Energy drained, Jana let her body become limp until a surge of the life force within her became strong once again. It was possible that Ashzar had not connected with her at all. She had been pulled back, stopped from communicating with him. Jana jumped to her feet, determined now to get to the bottom of all this.

Back on the bridge, Jana started to bark instructions to her Technical Engineer, but thought better of it. Instead she wrote the instructions on a scroll. The infra-red missiles needed to be made ready to fire upon her command. This function had not been taken away, probably because whoever was behind all this figured she wouldn't fire if there was nothing in her viewfinder to fire upon. Probably, every word spoken could be heard elsewhere and all caution needed to be exercised.

"1st Mate Technical - Fire 1! Fire 2! Triple the power and fire 3!

Watching the view monitor, Jana could see the missiles hit their target and explode. The turbulence rocked Jana's ship as at the same time the infra-red released from the exploded missiles brought the structure of a ship in view. It was massive.   Instantly the view monitor changed to show an angered look on the face of a man now on screen. Jana's sharp intake of breath could be plainly heard in the silence that now permeated the bridge of her ship. Jana could hardly get the name of the man past her angered, choked up throat. "DRAKE TRAITOR!!!"

The scowl on Drake Traitor's face turned to a menacing smile. "Welcome Jana. It matters not that you've been smart enough to detect my well thought out deceit. That's my girl." He clapped his hands slowly three times mocking her intelligence. "You've always been one of the most brilliant, not to mention Beautiful, women in the Pleiades. Ashzar should be proud of his protégé. Brilliance can only shine as bright as its teacher. And you, Jana Dear, shine so brightly – I spotted you a light year away. You fell right into my hands and I couldn't be a happier man. The replicated Solfatara star was set into place for the Mighty Ashzar. I'd thought to have to wait for eons for the man, but you my sweet, have given me the gift of time itself! You've made my work easier as I can now, how do they say….destroy two Gamma Quadrants with one thought probe." Drake Traitor laughed uproariously.

Jana opened her mouth to speak, but Drake Traitor cut her off as she was told, "Say nothing Jana. This journey is just about at its end and you are under my authority. All your questions shall be answered in due time." With this, the screen went into static mode and all systems shut down leaving Jana and her crew in pitch darkness.

Her 1st in command asked, "Commander, shall we turn on the kryptonic backup systems for lighting?" "No." Jana replied. "We'll need to save those for emergencies when we're somewhere out there under our own power. There's not much we can do just now except – sit tight and let this pitiful, mad excuse of a pleiadian play out his role of Captor. However, the glow lites from our belts can be used to light the way to your quarters if anyone feels the need to rest for awhile. Something tells me Drake Traitor doesn't intend this to be a short visit, but believe me, he's picked the wrong warrior to play games with this time. Obviously, he hasn't watched me too closely as we were growing up together. He's a weak man, but a weak man can be a dangerous one and that means I have to be very, very careful. I'll play along with him for now." Jana's 1st in command gave orders for the crew to retire to their quarters until systems were back on and then all were to return to their stations.

Jana was lying on her bed, arm slung across her face when she sensed someone in the room with her. Stilling her mind, she scanned the vicinity to try to locate a familiar energy source. Jana bolted upright to a sitting position. "You were not given permission to enter my quarters," Jana snapped. "I need no permission my Dear. You belong to me and if any permission for anything is to be given from now on it will come from me! I hope you understand that as I do not like repeating myself," Drake Traitor Growled. "Now on your feet!"

Jana didn't move. Drake Traitor smiled, snapped his fingers and moved from the room. Jana was yanked from her bed by two Big "UGLY" things. She was used to all sorts of beings. They came and went from her planet, but these guys were "UGLY" with snouts 12 inches long and she struggled to keep from fainting from their stench. One rubbed his hand-paw across her breast ripping the fabric of her uniform as she fought against her bondsmen. Drake Traitor laughed at her distress.

"Ashzar......Where are you," she mentally screamed as the nasty mouth (?) on the snout came down to claim hers before she passed out cold. When she awoke, she found herself in a beautiful room, but she was a prisoner in the room as the laser beams shooting across the entryway attested. Drake Traitor sat across from her watching her as she came around. She tried to sit up, but couldn't. Restraints held her in place. Cool air crossed over her body as she looked down at the unfamiliar attire. There was a band around her neck, burnt gold with azure gems inset. A matching band surrounded her wrist and ankles. A sheer piece of gauze-like material connected to the neck band was the only covering on her bronzed light body. Drake Traitor saw her looking down at her new garment and volunteered an explanation when her murderous eyes settled now on him. "How'd you like the little drama I set into place for your entertainment? The

"Runtle Snouts" are just an example of what could happen to you if you defy me Jana. Do you have any idea within that beautiful head of yours – just how long I've loved you? How long I have waited to see you look at me as I've seen you look upon Ashzar when you thought he wasn't looking? Can you imagine the torment you've caused me all these years when you could not get past seeing me for more than just a friend? Someone no more special than the cloned replicates that are deployed for doing all the menial tasks for the Quadrant? Well….NO MORE!!! From this day forward you are mine." He laughed again. "Let Ashzar come for you. Have no fear, my Dear. His brilliance will get him here. Enough of a trail was left to make him smoke his brain, but he'll unravel the clues and destroy Galaxies to get to you no doubt. And when he gets here, my love, you will witness his demise so that you will never challenge me as you've done countless others and you will never have the hope of Ashzar to ever again rescue you. His death will be final in your vision as well as in your mind. As for your attire…imagine Ashzar's anger when he sees how much of your beauty is revealed for my pleasure and for the pleasure of the whole Nissisoo Quadrant here in the outer realms beyond the black hole. Later you will be taken to the Crystal Auction Post and shackled there in plain view of anyone who by chance ventures into this lost Galaxy of the Universe. We both know that Ashzar will be our next visitor. You will be the reason he surrenders and not take up battle. You'd better hope you mean that much to him. I'm willing to gamble that you do. Guards! Take her to the post!

Drake Traitor bent to kiss her but Jana turned her head away. Placing a finger under her chin he turned her head back and his eyes were a pool of darkness as he gazed into hers. "*NEVER* do that to me again Jana. I will make you sorry." He stepped back from her, eyes never unlocking from hers as the guards released the rings from the bands on her body. Jana boldly spat at him, "I will see you dead before you ever touch me again Drake. Count on it!!!" Drake Traitor smiled, eyes glaring, as she was dragged away.

Jana was shackled to the Crystal Post, wind blowing the material that was hardly there. Humiliation such as she'd never before felt would make her survive this. She prayed Ashzar would not come. She did not want to submit him to this. "Stay away Ash. I can handle this," she thought. Anger was threatening to explode her brain. She worked at her bonds to no avail. "Don't come Ash, don't come. He'll be forced to cut me loose and I'll find a way to cut out his black heart." She yelled to the Universe, "Help Me..................!!!"

Fear was not something Ashzar was accustomed to experiencing and it sat like some evil obstacle in his mind. It was maddening to have the technology of a hundred worlds and be so helpless. As he stood on the command ship and called out to the Universe for some direction, he got the strange feeling that Jana was near. He strained mightily with his inner vision, but all he could detect was a faint feeling that she was near. The feeling faded as quickly as it came and left him even more confused.

"Deploy detector probes in all directions for half a light year," was all he could think of to say. Immediately his crew and ship responded and he had an array of information spread before him that was capable of detecting minute particles of organic matter as well as the faintest of energies in all known spectrums. Silence was thick on the bridge as scan after scan revealed nothing but the residue from the Solfatara star. Something was not right here, but he could not resolve anything in his mind that pointed in any direction.

Suddenly, a vision of horror flashed before Ashzar's mind. He could feel Jana and see a hideous snout pressing against her in a kiss. Revulsion boiled up inside him and as suddenly as it came, the vision was gone, leaving a foul stench in his mind. Drake Traitor! Such evil could only be attached to one such as him. Ashzar knew fear for the second time on this mission as memories of one so evil that he could not be reached by all the forces of light began to come to the surface. He was not afraid for his crew or ship, but for Jana. Love for her poured forth from the very core of his being as he tried to rid his mind of the revulsion caused by the images of Drake Traitor's servant touching her. A new sense of urgency overwhelmed him as he entertained thoughts of her supple young body in the grips of one so entwined with the forces of evil.

"Commander," called the second engineering officer, "Come and take a look at this." Ashzar studied the display of the far-field ion detector. To the untrained eye, it looked like beautiful colored waterfalls cascading down a bumpy screen. To Ashzar, however, there was a wealth of information about the faintest residual traces of energies in many spectrums. He could see the faintest spot in the infrared band near the event horizon of the nearest black hole. "Move the probe to within a million kilometers of that black hole and refine this data stream."

As the data on the ion detector continued its cascade, he was convinced that some form of energy weapon was responsible for the single spot that kept appearing. Since nothing known in this Quadrant could account for it, it had to somehow be connected to the explosion and Jana's disappearance. A quick mind link with his weapons staff confirmed his suspicions.

"Change course and skirt the event horizon of that black hole," he ordered. Immediately, the magnificent black hole seemed to jump onto the view-screen and fill space with its beauty. A scan of the main computer files showed nothing remarkable about this black hole. Designated QW-7686, the black hole before him was small and secluded. Suddenly as the angle between the ship and the event horizon changed sufficiently, an alarm blasted out across the bridge.

"Sir! There is a worm hole decaying rapidly on the far side of the event horizon. It was blocked by the hole itself." Without bothering to consider the consequences, Ashzar willed the massive Command Ship toward the worm hole. As the ship responded, they entered the decaying energy field at nearly the speed of light. Immediately, Ashzar realized that he had just risked everything for Jana. His second realization was that the black hole distorted the worm hole so that it passed through into another Universe. Energies assailed his senses as he drove his command ship at many times the speed of light. It appeared that in less time than could be measured, they had left the known Universe for someplace unknown. A quick mental scan of the instruments showed readings that made no sense at all. Ashzar paused briefly and searched this new region for signs of Jana. "She is here!" his excited mind yelled. Although the sensor arrays could detect nothing, he could feel her somewhere "out there". Forgetting for a moment where they were, he honed in on the trace of her energy and ordered the ship in fast pursuit of the phantom feeling of Jana.

CHAPTER 13
THE BREAK

J ana became angrier by the minute. The thought of being exploited and abused was more than her mind could handle. Out here in the middle of space unknown, she felt that even the "Exulted ones" could not hear her. Her cry for help would go unanswered, but Jana was taught by the best and the thought of Ashzar finding her this way gave her strength from unknown forces to find a way out of this dilemma.

She couldn't reach Ashzar through the power of mind, probably because he hadn't a clue to where she was and even his most technical genealogy trace system could not penetrate this God forsaken place. How could she have missed the evil strand that flowed through the Genetic patterns of Drake Traitor? She was outstanding in false energy reflexology. Ash had drummed this into her thought patterns over and over again. *Never underestimate the enemy.* How many times had she heard this one? Yet, Drake Traitor had been around them seemingly forever. If Ashzar had known he was this evil, wouldn't he have said something to her? That they were rivals – everyone was aware of that and Ashzar would berate her every time she was caught near him. But not once did he make her feel her very livelihood would be threatened by him.

No time for this kind of thinking. She needed to contact her crew. Once again Jana lowered her pulse rate and began deep breathing, in and out, reaching the energy level to leave her body. She scanned the area in search of her crew. Nothing turned up from her efforts inside the hideous looking space dwelling Drake Traitor obviously called his home. Grotesque was the word for this structure. Wait. Jana was picking up Marina. Beneath the structure…..must be some kind of dungeon under the dwelling. Jana honed in on Marina's energy pattern. Sure enough they were dungeons. UNBELIEVABLE! I thought these things only existed on Earth. Rather antiquated wouldn't you say Drake? Jana smiled at her own musings surprising herself since she was in such a desperate situation.

Finding Marina, she telepathically spoke to her. Marina looked in the direction of Jana's voice. "Marina. Are you and the crew alright?" Marina answered the affirmative. "Have you been strip searched at all?" Marina again answered the affirmative. Jana had to think quickly before her energy level began to wane. "Alright, get the others together. Use the energy of your minds as a collective group as I taught you to do back home. Overpower the minds of the guards. This is a little primitive I know, but it's all we have. Do you think you can do this?" Marina answered, "Quite definitely commander. Do you have any idea as to where they've taken you?" "At the mouth of this, this place - who knows what it is - is a crystal post right out in the open for all space travelers to see. I'm in quite a sorry state. You must get to me at once. My embarrassment is total. Ashzar must not see me this way. Time is running out. Here's what I'd like you to attempt. Find someone on this planet who looks as close like me as you can find. Bring her to the Crystal Post. Silence her in anyway that you must, but do not cause her any permanent harm. Take the stunners away from the guards you down and be careful when you approach the area where they have me. I am sure they will have it heavily guarded, but maybe not. We'll keep a positive outlook on things. I've got to go. I'm beginning to fade. You will know what you must do. Things are in your capable hands."

Marina was the best of Jana's crew, though all were top of the line officers. Marina possessed the above average intelligence, though, were mind connection was concerned. She and Jana worked endlessly with the other women until all could accomplish the out of body state at least for short periods of time.

Not only had the crew retrieved stunners from the guards, but modulated area diagrams also hung from the hip of one of them, making their escape slightly easier. There was some trouble along the way, but skirmishes were kept to a bare minimum. These Ladies were GOOD. Finding a Jana Look alike was no easy task though, mostly because most beings here were outcasts from other Galaxies and solar systems, but the Universe answered them as they unsuspectingly surrounded a female who threatened them with retribution from Drake Traitor himself. They couldn't have asked for a better replacement. Imagine Drake Traitor's anger when he retrieved one of his own from the Crystal post. The modulated scanner showed that the Crystal Post could be reached from underground. Not a lot of traffic was in these depths. Most people put here were left to rot. Skeletal remains were scattered everywhere. Marina was beginning to think this to be some kind of third dimensional world. How else could you account for Bones!

It didn't take long for the crew to work their way to Jana. The look on her face told the crew nothing and everything all at the same time. They knew better than to ever question her as to how she'd managed to get into this particular predicament. Quickly they switched Jana's clothes for the other woman's. Ashzar would know this wasn't Jana if he arrived because of his DNA Energy Technology. One thing bothered Jana though. This woman wore her clothes. The residue from her body would probably still cling to those clothes possibly fooling Ashzar into believing it to be Jana after all. No time now to ponder that. Jana hesitated. She looked at the woman and wondered if Ashzar would make the mistake. She'd kill him if he did! She grinned in spite of herself and moved to safety with the rest of the crew. The next line of action was to get to the ship. They had to be ready to move at exactly the precise moment. Their lives and Ashzar's and his crew depended on it.

A short time later the guards around the woman woke up. They noticed nothing different but couldn't understand why they were so sleepy. The woman would be out for quite some time. Jana's crew had seen to it. The guards thought her to be asleep, the wind blowing the gauzy material along with her hair across her face.

It didn't take long with the help of the area modulator to locate the docking bays. The first two bays did not hold Jana's ship. Luck was on their side with the third docking bay. There she sat as magnificent as she could be. The problem would be to board her unnoticed. Jana remembered she wore the other woman's clothing and hoped she could pull off the scheme running through her mind. "Commander! You're not going to try to tempt those guards out there are you? You can't truly be serious about this scheme I read in your head," Marina berated her. "Yes, Indeed I am Marina, but in case something goes wrong, use the collective mind altering technique just one more time. Hopefully, we won't need to do that. We all need to conserve our energy and strength."

Jana walked among the crew of Drake Traitor's landing pad. She shamelessly flirted and very quickly had all the men around her listening to the favors she promised the strongest man of the bunch. A contest would have to be waged of course. Each and every man was interested and soon the area where Jana's ship sat, stood empty. The crew very quietly went aboard capturing a couple mechanics in the process. Jana saw that all her crew was aboard and told the men that the contest would take place two days from today in this same area. "Don't let me down now guys. Goodness you are the most handsome hunks I've seen in a long time. I can't wait! Now get back to work before Lord Traitor has us all put to death." She smiled and sauntered off as if going away from the ship. She picked her shot and was on board ship in no time at all. Now all she had to do was wait for Ashzar to arrive in the vicinity of the planet. She wouldn't let him fight this battle alone. After all, she'd been the cause of this mess. It was the least she could do. Right now all hands needed to lie low. "Come on Ash," she thought to herself. "I need you, but you're going to need me too." She wanted to laugh out loud, but she'd save that for the Victory over Drake Traitor.

Ashzar was confused by all that was happening. Jana's disappearance, the Solfatara star exploding and then no trace of its existence and now the addition of his childhood nemesis into the equation. It was the most confused he had ever felt in his, so far, long and rich life. He assured himself that the crew was doing all that was possible with their instrumentation to solve the riddles and retired to his quarters to study the problem in solitude.

As soon as he calmed his mind, the background chatter rose to a level that reminded Ashzar there were many others who depended on him and who desperately needed his help. Parts of his mind automatically reached out to those who communicated with him. Most of these were on Earth and he allowed the mind links to form as thy sought and received answers to their perceived problems. He did his very best to impart to them that none were separate, that all are one. Over and over he encouraged them to look around themselves and know that all is the creator; that "love" was the only answer to all problems, that it was their choice to choose between the lighted path and the dark path and that their salvation was in their own hands. Yes, he was here to help as where so many, many others, but the brothers and sisters of the higher realms were bound by Universal Law to not interfere in the problems of man on earth unless they were called upon to do so. Even then, they could not stand between those humans of the lower dimensions and the lessons they had to learn. They could point them in the right direction, but the ultimate choice was theirs alone.

Usually, these channeling sessions were a balm for him, but today there was simply too little personal energy to allow him to get too deep into the conversations. As he shut out the noise, the location and possible rescue of Jana became like a bright light before him. His focus allowed him to concentrate entirely on the problem while his lesser brain carried on all the other functions required of him.

A beautiful meadow was an ideal place to rest. A fertile valley stretched away from Ashzar into the distance. The valley was ringed with low, wooded mountains and everything was in the splendid colors of fall. As Ashzar lounged in the meadow and looked out over the valley, he saw some new buildings off in the distance that he had never noticed in hundreds of visits to this meadow in his mind, his place to be, to think, to learn. He was aware suddenly that the buildings were arranged in the form of numerals on a clock. Shadows from the greatly accelerated passage of the sun formed the hands of a gigantic clock as Ashzar watched from his high meadow perch. Clocks? Here where time had little meaning and no use? Ashzar pondered the implications. Suddenly, he gave a physical start as he realized what the message he read in his meadow / mind was trying to convey.

Charging onto the bridge of the Command Ship, Ashzar began issuing orders and instructions to his crew. Within minutes the new search yielded results. "Sir!" yelled Narborivck from within the jungle of electronic and organic sensing consoles, "you were right; there is evidence of a major temporal shift in this region only hours before our arrival. Based on the speed and direction of the Molecular Particles we measured, something big passed thru and left this Universe entirely. My calculations indicate it is immediately parallel to this one and along the same approximate timeline."

Ashzar was very familiar with the theory that countless Universes existed in parallel with his own, just as multiple dimensions existed along the same timelines. He had been involved in many of the earlier Federation attempts to establish contact with those other Universes. After reviewing all of the readily available data, he, along with his closet advisors decided to attempt the impossible. Knowing exactly where the earlier temporal shift had occurred, they drove the Command Ship through the same region of space at exactly the speed of light and along the same trajectory as the existing tracks left earlier.

Countless energy assailed Ashzar's senses as the Command Ship seemed to shimmer for a moment and then the scene on the viewscreens went berserk. Familiar star patterns were replaced, colors shifted upward in spectrum and his head was filled with the thoughts of beings he never before had heard across the reaches of space. As he began blocking out the noise, one thought came across clear as a bell, "Ashzar, I need you......."

Jana! It had worked and she was here in this place. Immediately he ordered the ship to follow the previous trajectory and proceed at maximum speed. Honing his senses, Ashzar scanned the incoming flux of feeling and emotions, seeking clues to what awaited if and when he caught up with Jana.

CHAPTER 14
DESPERATION

J ana was becoming very nervous. Would Ashzar even come to this place? Would he be able to find it even with all his Universal expertise? Drake Traitor was the very essence of Evil. The name is certainly an appropriate one for the carnivorous being that he truly is. Drake, however, doesn't feed on flesh, but on the spiritual energy of goodness. Like the space vampire, he could not thrive without those energies. His aura was darker than dark. It was black and a being with a black aura was worse than the Earth Disorder termed cancer. The more you tried to dispel it, the more destructive it became. Only one with his immense foul energy could bypass the very boundaries of light to hide himself among one of the darkest regions of the Universe, then disguise and confuse the entryway to such a horrible existence as this. This place could quite possibly be the reality of Earth's mental bondage of Hell. Drake Traitor was that thing which pulsed and grew and grew. It was his energy that was alive within and around the Solfatara star. Only at this moment did Jana truly compute the danger she was in.

These thoughts brought to fore the conclusion that Ash would not come. Her heart swelled for him because she knew somewhere out there he was attempting, with every power available to him, to get to her. Such was his love for her. She smiled then because at times the man could be impossible! However, he fired her blood and she couldn't imagine having it any other way.

It was time to move! Already a trillion heartbeats of waiting had

passed. Not only might her crew be missed, but by now Drake Traitor might already know that it was not she at the Crystal Post.
Quickly Jana made the decision to make a run from the Nississoo
Galaxy. "All Hands!" she shouted. "Man your stations. Prepare for
lift off immediately. Run the check list verbally if you please."

Technical person….."All Systems go Commander!"

Navigator………….."Systems, here, in good order, Sir!"

Engineer……………"Commander, we have failure in the
booster ignition chambers. All levels of the power surge thrusters
are not in sequence. Someone has tampered with the Power Flow
Energy Scrimatons. Our sensor systems don't give a clue as to
where the problem lies."

Jana swore….."Flagensturr" (Oh Blessed Universe, I'm becoming like Ashzar without giving it any thought. Pray his strength
helps me through this). Just as quickly as that thought crossed her
mind her expertise at commanding her ship kicked in. "Bring me the
mechanics from the detainee cubic. That's who the culprits are
who've tried to sabotage the ship. At Drake Traitor's command, no
doubt. Damn that……"

"Going somewhere my Dear?" Murderous rage, issued forth
from the very deepest barrel of hell, spit each word at Jana to sink
like blades of slivered ice into Jana's heart. She knew no fear such
as the fear she felt now as she turned to face Drake Traitor. "How?"
Jana Began. "Silence!!! You intrepid piece of space carnage! You
dare to question my movements and you defy me even though you
were warned. You think that I am someone to be humiliated? You
think to make sport of my Authority? By the time I am through with
you….You'll crawl to me, Jana …..Daughter of Dakkar, Servant of
ASHZAR. The Crystal Post was nothing compared to the humiliation you will now experience."

Drake Traitor walked up to Jana and grabbed a hand full of hair
at the nape of her neck, jerking her head back until she thought he'd
snap the chakra's out of total alignment. He pressed a diamond Si-
cletron Blade at her throat and growled just one word….. "Walk!!!"

"Wait! Please," Jana Pleaded. "Drake, hear me I beg of you."
Drake Traitor smiled and waved a hand thru the air, gesturing to his
guards and mocking Jana at the same time. "Ah-h-h, she begs me.
At last she submits as is a She Dogs place. But you will not be

spared punishment as payment to your defiance. Speak!, and quickly before the taste in my gall becomes more bitter than you have already caused it to become."

"I do not care what you do with me. I will do all you ask, but please, set my crew free. This has nothing to do with them. They but follow my orders, pledged to me as by Pleiadian Law. This war is between me and you." Drake Traitor Roared. "And that Blood Monger ASHZAR!!!"

"Yes," Jana said in a low voice, "and Ashzar. Drake – release my crew and assure them safe passage back thru the Quadrant. I will be of no more trouble to you. You have my word as Commander of the Star ship Free Spirit."

Drake Traitor threw back his head and laughed aloud. "Her word. She gives me her word." The laugh changed instantly to a dangerous tick on one side of his face. "What kind of a fool do you take me for? Your *Word*????? When, Jana of the Pleiades, have you ever kept your word to anyone? To the incompetent Dakkar, who cannot handle his own daughter? To that space Vermin Ashzar who can't force the likes of you into a submissive mode? Spare me your falsity of pleiadian deception."

As Drake Traitor ranted on and on, Jana initiated mind link control with her crew. She spoke 1st with her Technical Advisor. "Lieutenant Kretomra, did you notice if the Frigid Freon Capacitator was still in working order? Fabulous. Listen closely everyone. I am going to try to get Drake Traitor and his guards within the Capacitator Range. Watch closely for my signal then activate the Detonation switch. It's our only chance."

Jana did indeed manage to lure Drake Traitor *and* his guards over to what should have been his doom. Jana gave the signal, but Drake Traitor saw what was coming and he screamed like an animal gone mad. His Guards were now frozen solid as liquid ice was soaked into their bodies via a refined mist perfected by Pleiadian scientist. Drake Traitor lost an arm in his effort to get free. He pulled his laser Gun and shot at Jana. Jana was not about to be under Drake's authority and she dived at the man's ankle to bring him down, but not before a laser beam pierced her right side. Drake Traitor leapt out of the ship as he'd no guards to back him and as Jana's crew helped defend their Commander.

"I'm alright Marina," Jana moaned. "Get us out of here. Still...have....the....Mechanic? Give 'em an ....ul...ti....matum. Get us....out........" Jana lost consciousness.

The crew did get the ship up and running. She was back in shape and picking up speed. Marina knew no time could be wasted in trying to break the time barrier to get through the worm hole. "Free Spirit" was headed directly into Ashzar.

Marina had the crew help her to get Jana to Sick Bay. Her goal was to make Jana as comfortable as possible as all medical equipment had been rendered useless after the blast from the Solfatara star. Without medical help, Jana would die. Marina refused to add substance to this known fact believing instead in the miracles the Universe bestowed upon those deemed worthy. Who could be more worthy of such a miracle than Jana? Marina creased her brow thinking back over the good, fun times she and Jana had shared and smiled as thoughts of the crazy antics Jana had pulled on her father and on Ashzar, presented a mental re-run of times past. Ah-h-h yes. Ashzar. Jana loved the man. As fiercely as she tried to pretend she didn't, Marina could see thru the false facade. Marina had been around her friend long enough to be able to pick up on her true feelings. Now was she to lose the one true friend she'd had since babyhood? No! Jana was strong. Perhaps therapeutic touch could be of some benefit here. She had to try. There was, however, no change in Jana's condition hours later. Her body was hot to the touch and Marina was forced to leave Jana in the care of the Universe. "Where are you Ashzar," thought Marina. "If ever your connection to Jana was needed, it's now." She needed to get back to the bridge to see what could be done to try to get back to familiar Quadrants. That in itself would take another miracle. To the Medical consultant she said, "Keep doing all you can do for the Commander. Let me know if there is any change. I'll be on the bridge."

Back on the bridge Marina looked out thru the portside and was greeted with nothing but blackness. There was not a star or beacon of light to be seen. What was this place she wondered, a worried frown on her face. It would definitely take a miracle to get them out of this forsaken hole. She shouted orders. "Send out a Missile Space Probe! We need to see if anything or anyone might possibly be within our trajectory. If this turns out to be positive within a peripheral radius of, say, 3,000 kilometers, we will then be able to communicate via the Telemetering Transmitters and hopefully the atmosphere here will enable our internal Satellites to give visuals on the Monitor Screens. In the meantime, initiate the Radar Tracking Systems and let's hope the equipment is powerful enough to ensure the reception of a reflected signal from any nearby Spacecraft in the instance that one might appear from an unknown wormhole after the Missile Probe has passed that vicinity."

"Captain Marina, Sir," the navigator volunteered. " The Accelerators on the Inertia Platform are showing changes in our velocity and position to a major Tracking Control Center. We are in the vicinity of another ship! I'm sure of it sir, however, I can't be sure if the visitor will hale as Friend or Foe, but it is so close we will know shortly. She approaches at 18,000 meters."

"Engage Retro Rockets to slow us down and hold her steady. Man your battle stations," Marina spoke calmly to her crew, "just in case the approaching ship is not an Ally. See if we have visuals and.....say a prayer to the Great Light Givers, Aton and Sananda. We need all the help we can get."

They soon had a visual though not close enough as yet, to make out the Markings of the on-coming Ship. She was moving at an incredible speed as if Demons were on her tail. Within seconds the Viewers Enhanced Projection Mechanism gave them a close up view of their Guest. Marina would know the huge Ship anywhere. ASHZAR!!!

Drake Traitor leered at Ashzar from the view-screen and his voice filled the cabin of the shuttle. "Ah-h-h, my old friend Ashzar, I suspect you are wondering what this is all about. Although I know that if I gave you a few minutes you could figure it out, but you do not *have* a few minutes. Do not attempt to break free of the energy beam that is disrupting all your systems. It is a little invention of mine that, like everything else I have done, was unnoticed. Nice, don't you think?"

Ashzar scanned the instrumentation on the shuttle control board and nothing was functioning properly. Slipping out from his console seat, he hastily moved to the rear of the shuttle and literally ripped a panel cover from the wall. Reaching inside, he carefully brought two ordinary looking crystals close together and the world dissolved.

As he brought the crystals into proximity, the inertia drive on the shuttle came to life momentarily and the shuttle was instantly moved many thousand kilometers away from Drake Traitor's huge ship. Instrumentation was back on-line and navigation showed a lock on his Command ship. Immediately he fired the conventional ion drive and keeping the Command Ship between the shuttle and the last location of Drake Traitor's ghost ship, he made his way back toward his ship. A quick scan of the computer record showed that the glimpse he had of Drake Traitor's ship was his alone, there were no readings to indicate that anything was amiss until all of the instruments failed.

Still struggling to understand how Drake Traitor could control his shuttle so completely, Ashzar brought the craft into the landing bay on the Command Ship. Immediately, he knew that he alone would have to make the attempt to board Jana's ship and solve the riddle of her whereabouts. A quick check with the bridge assured him that Drake Traitor's ship was not detectable on any of the operating scanners. He slipped into a ship's suit and cycled the airlock to the outside.

A ship's suit is one of the last places a person wants to be when traveling through space. There is enough oxygen supplied by the scrubbers to last about four hours and enough propellant for local maneuvering when doing outside maintenance work. Ashzar was hoping that whatever sensors Drake Traitor was using would not be triggered by his small mass in the suit and he carefully shut down all unnecessary electrical systems and fired his propulsion system to take him across the void separating him from the "Free Spirit".

As Ashzar drifted silently along toward the Free Spirit, he could make out a faint shimmer in the star-field where he knew Drake Traitor's ship was concealed. He strained to make out any damage on the exterior of the ship. Even with the aid of the suit optics, he noticed nothing obvious wrong with the Free Spirit. As he approached closer, he maneuvered slightly to place the mass of the Free Spirit between himself and Drake Traitor's invisible ship.

When he gently touched down beside the auxiliary airlock on the stern of the Free Spirit, the first thing Ashzar noticed was the obvious lack of lights. Ordinarily, the airlock areas were brightly lit, but this looked like a dead ship. He worked the mechanism to cycle the airlock, but nothing happened. He could sense that there was life inside and concluded that someone would have to manually operate the airlock from the inside. Removing a sonic spanner from the suit belt, he rapped on the airlock door. After what seemed like an eternity, a face appeared in the dimly lit door port and he turned on his suit lights hoping the person inside would not think him an intruder and fire a weapon. To his relief, he recognized the startled face of Marina and knew he would get inside.

The first thing Ashzar noticed as he stripped off the suit was how stale the air inside Free Spirit had become. Marina was talking a mile a minute and somehow he picked out the fact that most systems were either nonfunctioning or was on emergency mode only. His heart stopped for a beat as Marina stopped, covered her mouth with her hands and hysterically began talking about Jana being near death. Ashzar again attempted to feel Jana's energy but there was nothing. "Take me to her immediately!" Ashzar commanded as he mentally sent out waves of healing light energy directed toward wherever Jana might be.

CHAPTER 15
VISIONS

J ana's spiritual energy hovered above her body. She was used to leaving her body; however, she was not used to being "unable" to return to it whenever she had the mind to. This was not fun anymore. She was trapped here. Each time she tried to return to her body, she found she could not stay there very long. It hurt too badly. She did not have the strength to endure the pain and she found it hard to breathe there.

These bodies, being light bodies, were different from the heavy third dimensional ones. If wounded, one did not lose blood, but energy would seep from the light body rendering it useless. Depending upon the damage and therefore the rate of energy loss, sometimes telepathy could be attempted, sometimes not. Jana had been wounded badly and energy flowed from her body at an alarming speed. She was too weak to link mentally to anyone over a few breaths away. It would take someone with an intense rapid pulsing energy reserve to pull her through this dilemma. Things didn't look good at all for Jana and though she was gifted to keep a positive outlook on all things, she was about to lose that unique quality now. The silver cord which connected the spirit to the body was almost invisible now; just faintly there. She knew that when it disappeared her life force as she knew it, would become non-existent in these realms.

A spark of light just barely detectable to Jana flashed before her vision. "What was that," she wondered; her hope all but gone, but in that instant a burst of energy revived her spirit. Not knowing why, she began to float beyond the room where her body lay. As she moved away from her body she took a good long look at it. Her skin tone was a grayish tan, a very sickly looking pallor and it was so very, very still. Her heart went out to the girl she saw lying there, no longer recognizing the fact that it was a connection to herself. She floated thru the sturdy wall partitions that were made from a molecular material that Earth people still studied – trying to comprehend how the lightweight fibers stood up to its durability and trying everything within their capabilities to duplicate it. Nothing human-made could penetrate it and yet Jana passed thru as easily as the wind would rustle the leaves on a tree.

She moved along the halls of Free Spirit and saw a woman speaking to a man on a monitor. The room in which the Woman stood was in shambles. The picture on the monitor was statically breaking up and the conversation was not audible to Jana. The woman seemed agitated and the man looked distraught, a worried countenance on his weary face, though he did his best to keep the emotions hidden. She wondered why she was seeing these things; she wondered who these people might be. She then moved beyond the Free Spirit to occupy yet another space and she was somehow familiar with her surroundings and she was facing the man she'd just seen on the monitor just a second ago. He seemed hurried, almost running to exit the area he'd just occupied. She followed his every move, unsure of what the reason could be. She wanted to stop, but found she had no control and she had no will to fight what seemed to be inevitable. It was simply too difficult. Again, she vaguely wondered why she was here watching all this. The man and many others seated themselves within a small space craft of some sort. Jana wondered at the rush and where might their destination be. Whoosh!!! A millisecond and she was in yet another space watching another man. This man was like a caged animal pacing back and forth across an area that had all kinds of technological Data Streams feeding one to the other, like scientific tendrils of a living creature pulsing at exceptionally high energy levels and this man was Dark! There was something sinister in his carriage. Something evil in his features. Something black….no….void in his eyes.

Jana noticed that this man was different from all the other people she had seen. Different in appearance physically. One arm was decidedly strange. Electrodes ran from connectors around his shoulders into connectors attached to the arm. Bionics of some sort. She watched him smash a crystal with his fist which was covered with a black metallic looking glove. Expletives seemed to spew from his mouth and for the 1st time in what seemed like such a long, long time, Jana felt emotion. Revulsion, disgust and adjectives far beyond any of those.

Jana wanted to leave this place but she was not given that choice. She could only watch as the Dark one moved now to an exquisite Gem placed in the center of a molded gel like structure which protruded out of the floor to a height of about 4 to 4 ½ feet. The radiance of this Gem was blinding to the naked eye and Jana noticed the Dark one had placed visors over his dark eyes. He lifted it and leered sardonically at a monitor Jana had not noticed until now. She sensed rather than heard that this Gem gave the Dark one some special kind of power, though she had no idea why. None of this made sense and truthfully Jana didn't try to decipher any of it. She was tired, so very tired. She wanted to sleep. Just sleep. She was about to close her spiritual eyes when on the monitor she saw the handsome man she'd followed before being brought to this space. She sensed he was in some sort of danger and then she was back in the room over the sick girl's body and then she felt pain and everything went black…….

As Marina and Ashzar hurried through the shattered and disheveled Free Spirit, he could sense the energy and touch of Jana everywhere. He still could not sense her life-force energy although he knew if she were still alive she was within meters of him. He tried to ignore the destruction around him and focus his attention on collecting as much of his spirit as possible for the tasks ahead. He stopped short to avoid knocking Marina over as they came to a cabin door. Marina opened the door and he passed her to enter.

Jana lay on the bed and Ashzar's heart nearly broke as he still could not sense her energy. He knelt beside her and allowed his mind to reach out to her. He had already cut himself off from the multitude of multidimensional affairs he usually had going in his head and was able to focus all of his energy on reaching into Jana's body. He panicked as he sensed darkness and a lack of life. Suddenly, like a flicker at the edge of his vision, there was a faint trace of something. His mind locked onto it and followed it through her mind and as it strengthened, he recognized something horrible to his sensitive mind.

Loathing, as pure and simple as love or hate. This little spark filled Ashzar with a sudden rush of joy as he recognized that Jana was here because something was filling her with such loathing that it was overriding all her other emotions. Ashzar followed the synapses of her mind and felt her life-force flicker across his awareness. Suddenly, he connected with the flow of her unconscious mind and was stunned to see a picture more terrible then he could imagine.

Through Jana's extremely weak astral self, Ashzar could dimly see Drake Traitor hovered over one of the most powerful and rare devices the universe had ever known. The vision began to fade and Ashzar found himself drifting along with Jana as what little of her strength remained, was used to settle her mind into a deep coma. He pulled away from her, smoothing his path of withdrawal with a wall of golden healing light as his awareness returned to the room and the physical shell of Jana on the bed. He could not immediately still his mind as he searched for a clue to how Drake Traitor had obtained the holiest and most powerful mineral icon in the known Universe, the Lemurian Power Crystal from ancient Earth.

Ashzar regrouped his thoughts and focused on the most important task of the moment. Jana must survive. Ashzar would not admit it to anyone, but in addition to finding out what she knew about Drake Traitor and the Lemurian Power Crystal, he had a love for her that reached back across eons of time and he refused to admit that she could die. He focused his energy and slowly worked his way thru her body, paying particular attention to the areas where the dark stains of her injuries had spread. Millions at a time, he injected cells with life-giving energy and moved on to the next area. He had never encountered anything quite as foul as the illness spreading from Jana's wound.

Marina watched in amazement as Ashzar seemed to become unconscious himself while he sat next to Jana. The energy in the room had risen to a level that was obvious to even a lay healer. Great battles were being waged in front of her and the person she loved most dearly in the Universe was on the front lines. She added her own stream of healing power to those swirling around Jana's bed. As she felt her strength draining away, she could only silently pray that Jana would not make the great transition to the higher realms.

Marina had faced death many times and had seen many people die under a variety of circumstances. This was different. It was as if a piece of her soul were being snatched away as she imagined a life without the energy of Jana in it. "I must be dreaming", she was thinking as she thought she heard Jana's voice call her name. As she started awake, she realized that she had fallen asleep and she could still almost hear Jana call her name. Ashzar was asleep beside Jana's bed. His right hand was across her forehead and she did indeed seem to be breathing normally. She heard Jana softly call her again so she arose and went over to the bedside. Jana was either sleeping deeply or still unconscious.

"Yes, marina, it is me calling to you. I am still deep in a dream state as my light body and mental selves heal. I am calling to you to let you know that I am not leaving you, at least not yet. I saw in your dreams that you are unwilling to accept our parting at this time and I am here to reassure you that it is not the time. Rest well my sister." A fleeting image of Jana drifted across Marina's mind as her mind returned to the real situation and she hurried from the room to see if the Free Spirit could be saved.

As Marina entered the control room of the Free Spirit, she was amazed as every eye in the room turned to her and every motion ceased. She smiled slightly and could hear the audible releasing of breath as everyone breathed out at the same time. It did not take an expert to read the relief on her face and the crew members knew at once that Jana was still alive. As a hundred questions came at once, she simply stated, "Our mission now is to survive with this ship. Status report! All stations, now!"

There was a cool breeze blowing across the ruins as Ashzar drifted through a world without time. He recognized the ancient city of Ghardhuin on the planet Dur. It was a favorite dream state destination when he needed to be alone and rest his spirit. He knew in his mind that time on every level was suspended for him as he slowly wandered among the ruins and marveled at the play of light from the twin suns overhead. It was quiet here, no beings disturbed the calm energy of this abandoned city, no issue was pressing enough to intrude on the solitude. Ashzar was slowly playing over the events that led to Jana's near death and looking for meaning to the discovery of the crystal in Drake Traitor's possession. No emotions were allowed to interrupt his careful review of the events. He was at rest and was able to objectively look at what had happened. The universe obligingly added in some of the missing pieces and he began to understand what had happened, at least on a physical level.

After Marina's and Jana's mental telepathic communication and Marina left the room, Jana focused now on Ashzar. Their energies locked and Jana's Astral body walked toward Ashzar. She was so overwhelmed in feeling his energy that she took his hand and placed it on her face, lovingly stroking it as if she'd never let it go. She gently placed his hand by his side and placing both of her hands on his face, said "Thank you Ashzar. Thank you so very much for not giving up on me. I am who I am and so I shall not make excuses and I shall not apologize as I feel deeply that there is nothing that happens in the Universe without reason. There were lessons that I needed to master and a truth that I needed to acknowledge on an inner level. It was meant for you to join me here in these astral realms so that I could speak the truth of what I have learned. I don't know if I will ever speak these truths to you again, but it is your right to know them; to hear them. Your energy is a crucial part of my very existence and in the weakened state I find myself in, only you could give the energy needed to heal me; to bring me out of this space. Only you have the power to assuage my pain. I can move beyond here now, for you've paved the way with a path of golden healing energies. I will emerge strong in spirit though still weak bodily as your energies, connected with mine, reassemble the damaged cells. All will be well." She repeats softly, "All will be well."

Jana drew his face down to her own and kissed him with all the feeling she had within her very existence. Ashzar could not resist and would not forget the feeling she injected into his being at that very moment. She opened her very soul to him and he withdrew to the City of Ghardhuin, those ruins were he'd retreat to find solitude; to find peace; to feel pleasurable happiness. He needed to distance himself for a moment from Jana. He needed time to allow all the pent up feelings for Jana, long kept deep within himself, to accommodate the inner storm that was threatening to swallow him whole.

Ashzar sat on the steps of the ruins marveling at the play of light from the twin suns overhead, sidestepping his real reason for retreating here; not wanting to explore or accept what Jana's kiss had made him feel. He allowed his mind to play over the events that led to Jana's near death and looked for meaning to the discovery of the crystal in Drake's possession, but he would not allow his mind to rest on the power of Jana's kiss. Unbeknownst to Ashzar, his heart was wide open and in his parting he left a trail of blinding light in his wake. Jana followed easily and she gave him space sensing his need to come to terms with feelings so powerful that if not harnessed correctly....could well destroy them both. He must accept this, however, and it must be done here within the astral realms, among the dream state. Their hearts would become one heart from this time forward, ties irrevocable – and if only subconsciously accepted.......they would always know on some deep, deep level.

Jana walked from behind a column of the ruins that Ashzar sat facing. She was dressed in a sheer, white, Grecian style gown trimmed in gold. There were cut slits from the hem of the garment to her upper thigh and she was like a dream within a dream as she moved sensuously toward Ashzar. At first, because of the light from the twin suns, she appeared to be an apparition of pure energy; a blazing, glowing fire, but as she moved closer her body took on shimmering effects as though the sun had sprinkled golden stardust which attached itself to the ethereal aura. Jana gently lifted Ashzar's hands away which were clenched together as one might do when deep in thought and then she sat on his lap and kissed him again long and deeply. The ritual that followed sealed them together for Eternity. Removing her arms from around his neck, Jana arose after what seemed like forever and lifting her arms to point towards the twin suns she spoke with firmness and conviction, yet with a tone that sent shivers along Ashzar's spine.

"To the Universe I speak my truth to reverberate through every Dimension, every Solar System, every Galaxy......I pledge my love, my heart, my soul to this man Ashzar. So shall it vibrate in the never ending circle of oneness. Together we shall be a power in allegiance to the Givers of Light. I pledge my very life to your service." She turned and faced Ashzar so that she could drink in the goodness of his aura and said, "I love you Ashzar as the Universe is my witness. So be it." She turned back to face the twin suns. Lightening flew from her fingers to encircle the Suns and clouds covered them. The wind blew as though a storm was about to wage war. Broken pieces of the ruins flew past them at frightening speeds while uprooted brush rolled beyond sight. Jana's hair whipped about her face as she turned once again to Ashzar and pointed her finger at his heart.

A jolt of love brought Ash to his knees and Jana Knelt beside him laying her head on his shoulder. Electricity jumped around their bodies like a live wire torn loose and hanging from a powerful space transistor. Ash enfolded Jana within his arms, then, picking her up he retraced his path back to the entrance of the astral realms and sat her gently upon her feet. Holding his hand, love shining in her eyes she said, "We will remember this within. See you on the Free Spirit."

Jana moved her head, a slight moan escaping her lips. Ashzar woke immediately and was holding her hand as she opened her eyes. "Ashzar," she spoke softly and looked into his eyes. Something was different there which filled her in some way; a difference that made her feel elated. Ashzar was thinking along the same terms as he looked into her eyes. The memory of what they'd shared eluded them for the Universe would bring bits and pieces to their conscious scopes at the proper time. The seed had been planted and would sprout for the connection shared at that moment was enough for now.

CHAPTER 16
REUNION

Ashzar awoke and found himself staring into Jana's eyes. A feeling began welling up inside him and at once he masked it. He had always known that he loved Jana, but he had never felt such raw love, such a desire to hold her. A vision of Jana in a beautiful white sheer gown drifted across his consciousness and he felt the feelings go even deeper.

"Welcome back Jana", he spoke softly. "I rarely feel fear, but you certainly gave me a shock this time. Is there anything I can do for you?" Jana smiled weakly and searched behind his eyes for recognition of what she was feeling. "No," she responded, "I am weak, but I will survive."

Suddenly, like a blast from a laser, memories of the past few hours' events came rushing back and she stifled a scream. Ashzar, sensing that she was suddenly distressed, spoke softly again. "You rest, doctor's orders. I am going to the command bridge and see if Marina needs a hand. I also need to communicate with my ship. Rest and summon me if you need anything."

Ashzar got up and left the room suddenly. He did not trust himself any longer in the same room with Jana. Too many new feelings and emotions, too much history between them, and too many voices reaching out for help within the shattered hulk of the Free Spirit. He made his way to the command bridge and was stepping through the door when the first jolt of the ship nearly knocked him down.

Ashzar recovered his balance and shut out the screams of the injured. He quickly scanned the command bridge and saw that almost nothing was working. Marina was yelling about an unknown energy source, the navigator was trying to stop a nasty gash from bleeding energy (which was a bluish light source) all over the console and the air quality seemed suddenly worse if that was possible.

"Marina," Ashzar called, just loud enough for her to hear. "What hit us and where did it come from?" Ashzar knew from whence it came, the sinister energy of Drake Traitor permeated the energy blast. The Lemurian Crystal was a very powerful weapon in the hands of one bent on dark destruction and it was obvious from this latest assault on the Free Spirit that the energy blast was intended solely to destroy.

Ashzar immediately made mental contact with his First Officer aboard the Command Ship and searched for clues about the location and intent of Drake Traitor and the crystal. They had detected the blast milliseconds before it struck the Free Spirit and were attempting to track the origin. Ashzar knew that the information was already too old to help them escape another attack, but perhaps a pattern would emerge. Surely Drake would move his ship to a new location prior to attacking again and each attack would be a surprise.

Ashzar was so absorbed with telepathic conversations back and forth about the next possible attack that he didn't see Jana make her entrance onto the bridge. He looked up from a 5D strategic map being generated by the computer and was shocked to see her peering down at his table from the command platform. She was pale, almost gray after her ordeal, but Ashzar was pleased to see that the fire of life burned strongly in her eyes and her aura was beginning to clear and take on its original look of strength and complexity.

"Jana, it is too soon for you to be here, rest more." Jana responded, "Sorry Bud, but this is my ship and I am responsible for the lives of this crew. We will meet this together as one, united, to escape this attack. I will be here and you must accept that." Ashzar nodded in respect to the power of her words which far exceeded their simple meaning and looked back at the map he was generating. Suddenly, a burst of mental energy from his Command ship alerted him to another wave of energy streaming toward the Free Spirit. Before he could shout a warning, it struck.

If there was damage to the Free Spirit before, there was mega damage now. The Free Spirit definitely could not take on too many more attacks of this magnitude. Though weak, Jana's mind was surprisingly sharp! Screens of information moved rapidly through her mental vision. She had no idea where it was all coming from or how she came in possession of this knowledge, but her feelings were strong, and she'd been taught to trust her instincts and she'd been taught by the best! Jana knew exactly where Drake Traitor kept his crystal. She had an idea. She'd put her idea before Ashzar and hopefully Ash could build upon it.

Knocked on her hands and knees from the most recent blast, body crying out against the assault, Jana reached for the strong hold surrounding the Command platform to pull herself up from the floor. There were tears forming in her eyes from the sheer exertion of forcing her body to move towards Ashzar. Ashzar's immediate thought after the attack had been to search out Jana to ascertain her condition. When he'd locked her in his vision and saw her plight, he quickly went to her aid, cursing himself because he knew that at all cost – his first priority should have been to do whatever was needed for the safety of the entire crew. That was Pleiadian law and he'd taken an oath to that effect! But seeing the excruciating pain Jana was obviously in, priorities dissipated as soon as they would emerge. He'd also taken a solemn oath to Dakkar to protect his daughter with his life! He'd almost broken that promise once, though it was beyond his control, dang if he'd take the chance on losing her again!

Gasping for breath Jana laboriously half spoke, half whispered to Ashzar, "Ashzar….Please…..listen. Drake Traitor…..crystal." Ashzar interrupted her to tell her what he'd read within her subconscious when she was in her comatose state about the crystal. From that information he knew exactly where the Lost Lemurian Crystal was located on Drake Traitor's ship. Jana nodded to affirm his information and began again, having had time to gather more strength while Ashzar reviewed her spiritual aided visions.

"Remember long ago when you taught me to use the energy of the mind to make manifest Cause and Effect? It occurred to me that Drake Traitor always wanted to know why we were always closeted so much and what it was that we did in those mandatory sessions. I have a hunch that while he may be brilliantly intelligent, he never stayed still long enough to utilize the benefits of Mental Molecular

Energy. I heard you say that he cannot hear you when you speak telepathically to your crew and thinking back, he did not pick up on me and my crew when we used telepathy to escape from the planet Nississoo. If he "can" use telepathy, our frequencies must be stronger or he simply cannot cut into our frequency mode patterns. It's clear that when confusion surrounds him he doesn't concentrate. He loses Focus. So my thoughts are that I could spar with him across the monitor, further reducing his concentration as your crew mentally scrambles the mental state of Drake's crew. His entire crew mentally shut down leaves Drake a virtual target. This is where you come in Ash." Jana hesitated; worry creasing her brow before quickly going on. "You, then, need to get to Drake. There is only one problem within my scope that I can see and I honestly don't know what to do to get around it. Our Monitor isn't working and I need to get to your ship. Have I made any sense to you at all Ash?" Weak from the extensive exertion of even trying to talk, Jana leaned into Ashzar's huge frame for support. Ashzar scooped Jana into his arms as he issued Commands to Jana's crew.

"Keep your mental channels on alert for my signal! The outcome of this strategy depends upon the synchronicity of our combined forces and I will explain the plan to you and my crew only once for we haven't much time. Marina! I need your help in Moving Jana to the shuttle bay while we figure out how to return to my Command Ship." With long strides, Ashzar exited the Command Bridge taking great care with Jana's comfort. Once beyond the Automatic doors Jana said to Ashzar, "Ashzar, I think I can walk now. Please, let me try.

CHAPTER 17
GUILT AND BETRAYAL

Ashzar was relieved that Jana did not require much assistance on the long trip to the shuttle bay. Apparently the damage to the Free Spirit was not severe enough to knock out the gravity field, so it was possible for her to walk normally with an arm around his waist and him with an arm around her shoulders. Marina trailed along behind observing the two in the dim emergency lighting.

The shuttle bay was in relatively good condition when compared to the rest of the ship. Only blank wall screens gave an outward sign of the massive destruction elsewhere on the ship. Ashzar immediately contacted his First Officer and quickly, mentally relayed a summary of what was happening and the immediate need for a shuttle. After a few minutes consultation, they had a plan.

Ashzar came to Jana and sat with her. He could instantly tell that she was still not nearly one hundred percent, but was no longer in danger. She made small talk for a minute about the events of the past few hours and then looked up into Ashzar's eyes and said, "It's different now, you know." Ashzar was startled by the statement and said, "Yes, now I know exactly where Drake Traitor is aligned and what is truly in his heart."

Jana turned away and waited a long while before she quietly said, "You are the smartest person I know, yet you can be so damned stupid."

The little light in Ashzar's head was just beginning to flicker when a mental communication informed him that the shuttle had ar-

~ 122 ~

rived from the Command Ship. Ashzar wanted to know what stupid thing he was being accused of this time, but further personal discussion with Jana would have to wait for a more convenient time as they quickly cycled the airlock and boarded the shuttle. Without knowing why, as Jana looked out the view port along the length of the Free Spirit's hull, tears formed in her eyes and she knew that from this moment on, life would never even be close to the same.

She moved away from this reality and went within to allow herself to feel the anguish of the millions of thoughts floating through her sub-consciousness. This trip had been so very unlike any she'd experienced ever before. The Free Spirit was ruined, not beyond repair, but she had never been as brutally battered as she'd experienced on this escapade.

This was no child's play. People had been wounded severely and all due to her willful desire to irritate Ashzar. She'd run up against and fought the Universe's most evil adversary with no thought to the repercussions that such unwarranted actions could bring to the fore. The childhood friend she'd thought she had in Drake Traitor turned out to be the most vile, disgusting creature Jana had ever had the misfortune with whom to interact. She realized deep within that she'd actually helped this creature deceive the fine beings who inhabited the Pleiadian Star Clusters. Perhaps not knowingly, but it made her no less guilty.

She had help Drake Traitor by letting him use her small shuttle Craft from time to time, being sworn to secrecy as he'd explain some fabrication, suddenly made up in his mind, to draw attention from the true reasons he needed the craft. She, knowing he was forbidden clearance to operate these craft, thought it an absurd rule and would help him anyway for no other reason than to defy her father and Ashzar. Fun and games. That's all it was to her. She would get him special permission passes to access some of the facilities that were "off limit" compounds. Only a very trusted few ever had the authority to enter these and they were always well guarded. Now she knew the reason for the secrecy was to keep things that could be dangerous to the populace of their planets, out of the hands of some unscrupulous being such as Drake Traitor. Childish pranks, she'd thought. Oh how very wrong she'd been. She was no better than the scum she now wished to destroy.

Jana's burden was heavy. She had betrayed the very people she loved with all her heart. And Ashzar! Just when she'd come to terms with her feelings for him! How could she ever face this man again, let alone expect him to return those feelings if he knew the extent of her betrayal.

Returning to reality, Jana broke into outright tears. A down pouring of pain unlike that of any pain ever experienced in her long, long life. This was beyond physical or ethereal pain. This was pain of the soul. This was something clutching the feelings and emotions of her very existence and wrenching them from her life-force. This was true death for she knew she could never return home.

Ashzar was not used to such a display of emotion of this kind from Jana. He was caught off guard not knowing exactly what was or should be expected of him. He was not trained for this. This was not any of the rigorous teachings he'd been subjected to in his highly accredited life and he therefore did not know the defenses he should use to break down this new barrier erected suddenly before him. "Jana," Ashzar spoke softly. "Are you in pain? We are almost at the docking pad of my ship. Immediate medical attention will be waiting as soon as we arrive. Can you hang on a little longer?"

Jana wiped her eyes with the sleeve of the garment she still wore when she'd exchanged clothes with the woman from the Nississo Quadrant. She took a deep breath, resolve and resignation showing clearly on her flawless face. She held her head high and squared her shoulders knowing she could not let Ashzar know of her new plans. She looked him in the eye then and said to him, "High Commander, I am fine. Do not worry so over me. Forgive me the outburst. This is definitely not the time. I simply revisited the recent past horrors and I became overwhelmed. I do not require medical attention. I feel more strength now than I have felt in quite some time. My future requires it of me. We have much to accomplish this day, you and I. I will not let you down and I will never be the cause of your embarrassment and humiliation. Thank you for all that you have done for me. I shall never forget it." Or *you*, she thought to herself. "High Commander, I request permission to accompany you when you take Drake Traitor under Universal Arrest. I could serve as a breathing decoy. Close contact might be preferable to an unfeeling monitor. The monitor ploy would make Drake Suspicious."

Ashzar was taken aback for the second time in milliseconds. Jana had never, that he could remember, followed the required Galactic Rule which demanded he be addressed as "High Commander", a title bestowed upon him by the Tribunal Counsel due to his stature as Supreme Commander of the Entire Pleiadian Space Fleet just under the Authority of Esu Immanuel Sananda. He waived this preface of the title, however, to those closest to him....his crew and those other fleet units who had earned his respect. But Jana had never even called him commander, even when he threatened to turn her in to the Tribunal for her Heterodoxy willfulness! Something was not as it should be here. She needed to be closely watched. Perhaps it was side effects from her injuries. Her eyes lacked the fiery luster they usually held. Something was definitely amiss. He'd been too preoccupied to tune into her subliminal mind patterns and he truly needed all his attention directed to the task at hand. He resolved to tune into her thoughts as soon as this emergency was seen to completion.

Jana waited for an answer. She took the time to read Ashzar's thoughts and her heart went out to him. How she loved this man. She'd counted on his efficiency to tackle important issues first and knew he'd keep his mind concentrated on the dilemma they faced. Once the danger was over, she'd shut her mind down so that Ashzar could not read her. It was imperative that she do so. "High Commander Sir, you have not answered me................"

CHAPTER 18
RETREAT

Ashzar stared a moment too long at Jana before mumbling a halting "we shall see when it is time, I must work the plan through to conclusion." He could not remember ever seeing her in such a condition and was confused by all the signals he was getting from her. She appeared to be recovering quickly from her ethereal physical injuries, but it did not take close observation to see that something was amiss. Ashzar resolved to spend a moment probing the situation. The shuttle's arrival to the Command Ship docking bay disrupted his plans to look into Jana's situation and he was suddenly faced with the million things that must be done to put a manned craft into space, even more so in an emergency.

The journey to the Command Ship, while extremely stressful was nonetheless uneventful. Ashzar wracked his brain for a solution to the problem of getting out of this twisted hole in the Universe and returning to the known Universe, with the Command Ship and Free Spirit. He mentally dispatched orders to send a crew to Free Spirit to hasten the necessary repairs. His plan to move the shuttle along the shadow of the Free Spirit to avoid detection by Drake Traitor seemed to work. Always on his mind during the trip was Jana's ethereal physical and mental condition.

Jana sat quietly and watched as Ashzar piloted the shuttle into the bay with a fraction of his resources and planned with the rest. She admired his ability to focus entirely on a problem until the proper solution was found. She also regretted that during these periods he was not available to her. No matter, Jana was patient or at least that is what she always told herself.

Life on the Command Ship was its normal hustle and bustle. Because of the emergency, few of the crew members were in their quarters. It seemed as if the closed environment of the ship was entirely overcrowded as crew members scurried around on unknown missions. Ashzar didn't hesitate to guide Jana to the healing room and when she balked, he insisted that she at least allow the Medtech, Konvaser, to look her over. When she was finished and allowed to leave after a thorough physical, he was gone.

Ashzar was mind-linked with his closest advisors aboard the Command Ship. The immediate problem was simply that the Lemurian Crystal must be taken from Drake Traitor before he could learn enough of its powers to be a threat to the Galactic Federation. The risks were too high to assume that Drake Traitor would stay in this alternate Universe and leave the populated ones alone. There was a sinister purpose to his madness that must be stopped regardless of the cost to Ashzar and his ship.

Jana was irritated by the fact that she had to endure the medtech's delicate handling of her person. Probably due to the fact that Ashzar would have his head if he left even one small stone unturned. He was very thorough and this thoroughness was costing Jana precious time. She gritted her teeth more than once to prevent herself from raking him over the coals. When he stated that he'd report his findings to Commander Ashzar and then suggested she needed more rest – Jana lost the little composure left to her and snapped, "DON'T!" The Medtech lifted an eyebrow as if in thought and Jana quickly readjusted her attitude and speaking softly, hoping to avert him from her frazzled mental state, said, "Really, Konvaser, there is no need to concern the Commander at this time. He has more than enough to contend with and besides, I am quite fine. However, I will take your advice and lie down for awhile, I promise. But, if you have no objections, I'd rather go to my own quarters here on the ship and rest there. I'm sure I'll be more comfortable there in more cheerful surroundings.

Konvaser hesitated then said, "Alright. But I will check on you periodically to satisfy myself that you are as well as you seem to think you are, Jana. One should always expect the unexpected. After what you've endured, a period of convalescence is imperative."

If eyes could kill, the medic would no longer be among the living. Quickly shuttering the stare, though it did not go unnoticed by Konvaser, Jana replied with a falsetto smile, "Suit yourself. The time you waste will be your own. 'Til later then," and she stepped out of the infirmary.

Jana hurried to her quarters to shower and change into attire befitting her rank. There was always a wardrobe on board Ashzar's ship due to the fact that she always seemed to be on assignment to one place or the other with the man. Though she hated to admit it, there was always excitement on these missions with Ashzar, but things were different now and there was no time better than the present to put those things behind her.

Stepping under the Automatic Body Blower and donning the Fleet Commander Space Jumpsuit, Jana hastily pulled a brush through her hair and knotted it at the nape of the neck. She laughed out loud as she realized she'd been barefoot up 'til now and pulled a pair of stretch boots up to the Mid Calf of her shapely legs. A small pair of Starfleet bars, usually worn on the shoulders or breast of a suit, had been made into earrings and she placed those quickly in her earlobes. Reaching for a laser gun on a top shelf in her boudoir made her suddenly bend over in excruciating pain. She steadied herself and took a couple deep breaths until the pain subsided and mentally berated herself for being so careless. Reaching was something she needed to remind herself not to do. The area under her arm down to her side was still tender and she must not let anyone know, lest she be grounded. Strapping on the laser, her beaming device and her communications clip, she was now ready to find and confront Ashzar.

Reaching the Bridge, Jana scanned the room not locating the Commander. No one noticed her presence as everyone was busily seeing to the task Ashzar had set before them. Jana walked over to the Communications Officer and demanded to know Commander Ashzar's whereabouts. The officer looked at Jana rather uneasily and said, "Commander Ashzar has given strict orders that no one is to interrupt him until he gives the authority."

Jana smiled and said, "You do honors to your Commander in dedicating yourself to the task of carrying out his every command,

and, that is how it should be. However Lieutenant, you have not an-swered my question and I am giving you a direct order to do so, sir."

Ordinarily, Jana would have hated to pull rank, but at the mo-ment her mind was pointedly focused on Ashzar and she was at a point of no return. A mission known only to herself and a mission she'd no choice but to see thru to fruition. Once she had the infor-mation as to where Ashzar was sequestered, she boldly walked into the private officers meeting quarters.

The glare that Ashzar shot at Jana was matched equally by the glare Jana shot back at Ashzar. Before he could speak Jana inter-jected, "High Commander, Sir....I have vital information for this counsel and I shall not be put aside for one moment longer. I will accompany this expedition with or without your approval. I would hope that the latter would be your final decision. It truly would be the best for all concerned."

The thunderous look on Ashzar's face would have been enough to make the average man apologize for his rash behavior and seek some semblance of a face saving measure. However, Jana was not the "Average Man" and though inside she may have wished she'd approached things differently, she would not outwardly back down now. And Ashzar knew this...........

CHAPTER 19
THE PLAN

Ashzar was taken aback by Jana's brash behavior. He knew she had been injured seriously in the assault on the Free Spirit, but he assumed she would not have been released from medical without being fit for duty. He was not used to her formal attitude and had no time to deal with impetuous women on HIS Bridge. "Commander, this is neither the time nor place to hold this confrontation!" he hastily shot in her direction.

"I quite agree, Sir. However, this is not a confrontation; it is simply a statement of fact on my part as to my intentions." Jana used as much force as she could muster as she stated her case while the other officers watched in amusement. One new officer, however, was not used to these exchanges between Ashzar and Jana and stated his perplexity over the matter to another veteran officer who was seated beside him. "I can't believe he actually allows such an obstinate disregard of his stature from a mere woman; Commander or not. After all he *is* her superior. Does she have a death wish or what?" The veteran officer laughed and whispered, "You are new here, and so, let me give you a friendly piece of advice. These two have been railing at each other for as far back as I can remember. Don't ever, I repeat, don't ever let the Commander know for one moment that you look upon Commander Jana as a "mere woman." Trust me, my friend, you would see a demotion long before he'd ever think of demoting her. Those two have a thing for each other and everyone who's been around long enough knows that. And another thing,

Commander Jana can hold her own to any man and has earned everyone's respect. Just relax and watch the show. It can be a welcome respite from the normal, tedious day to day activities. Besides, I guarantee you she'll have something of some importance to say if the High Commander will hear her out. That woman has many, many times saved the day when everyone else was out of options."

Ashzar paused briefly and Jana could see he was using an ancient relaxation technique before he continued. "Jana! Enough! There are forces and consequences at work here far beyond your considerable capacity to understand. It will interfere with the execution of my plan if I have to deal with an officer that is not one hundred percent. You are not to attempt to join this party attempting to retrieve the crystal from Drake Traitor. Your presence could jeopardize the entire mission and I will not allow that."

Jana exploded with fury and intensity that physically shook Ashzar. "Who in Hell asked you to come chasing after me and rescue me? Who in Hell asked you for anything at all? You prance around the Pleiadian System like you own it. You take over running the operations around Earth like it was your individual pet project or something. Well, let me clue you in, High Commander. I am the Daughter of Dakkar, the most powerful legislative figure in the known Universe. I earned these Commander's Bars and I will be damned to being Drake Traitors concubine if you think you can run my life and tell me what to do! Oh, I know you technically have more rank than me, I know you and my Father are very close, I know you think that wisdom gives you privileges, but you ain't telling this warrior how to fix her own mess!"

"And furthermore, you need to learn that there is more to life than following your damn rule book. You are one of the coldest and most callous men I know, and despite what you might think, I know plenty of men....manly men who know a little about life outside of a fancy classroom or off the bridge of a fancy ship! You think you know so damned much? You think you have some right to tell me what to do?" Jana picked up a Throm Disk from the table and hurled it in Ashzar's general direction as her fury boiled to the surface.

He was immediately on his feet and deftly moved into a position facing her in order to restrain her if the violence continued.

"You think I'm mad? Huh? Well you wouldn't know mad or

crazy if it smacked you upside the head, Commander! Come on, "Uncle Ash", I dare you to lay one hand on me…" Jana spat her words at Ashzar and collapsed into a chair. She was dead tired but she knew she must remain strong for a few more minutes, just a few more. She carefully turned her head away so he could not see the tears beginning to collect in her eyes.

Ashzar paused too long before continuing, "Commander, I order you to report to medical immediately and remain there until released by the Chief of Medicine. I shall attribute this outburst on your injuries and forget your insubordination."

Jana sat with her back to Ashzar and silently prayed she could choke back the sobs for a while longer. As she summoned her energy inward and steeled herself for the next round, it occurred to her that perhaps she was a bit hasty in confronting him this way, cunning and craftiness could get her further than fighting ever would. She kept her head lowered and in a small voice said, "You are right, High Commander. I – I am not myself and ask your forgiveness. I shall return to medical at once. Thank you for your concern."

"That's more like it Jana," Ashzar said softly. "I could never forgive myself if something happened to you that I could have prevented. Go now and let's forget what was said here in anger today."

Jana fumed even more at his lack of resolve to fight with her, but the ploy was exactly what she needed to leave this room and begin the process of obtaining the Lemurian Crystal herself. "I'll show him! While he is planning his careful assault, I can complete the mission and be back before he even misses me." As she muttered these thoughts to herself, she could feel the beginnings of a plan taking shape in the recesses of her mind.

Ashzar sat in the briefing room saddened by the confrontation with Jana. It only took a few seconds however, for the matter at hand to slip back to the forefront of his mind and he continued planning the assault on Drake Traitor, unaware that Drake Traitor was not his number one priority, at least for the moment.

Ashzar had definitely overstepped his bounds this time. The incurable Cur. How dare he dismiss her, once again, as though she were nothing more than a babe still wet behind the ears! Of course he honestly felt that any decision he made was for the best of all concerned and Jana knew he took that responsibility seriously. Grudgingly she conceded to the fact that she admired him for the strength of his convictions. But his rules of steel were exactly that of a chauvinistic Fool! His intelligence, pride and ego stood between him and another possible Avenue to resolving the urgency of the situation. He'd never once considered assessing the vital information Jana offered to him and his most trusted advisors. No matter how often a female proved success in ways other than Brute Force, still they were considered inferior. Common decency, if for no other reason, would demand that she at least be heard. Well – she'd given him the opportunity to gain access to the most important factor of the entire counter attack. Without it the crew and all involved, including the crew of Drake Traitor, would die and no one fathomed a clue that they'd be walking straight into a hornets nest without this one very important element that was omitted from their Universal Knowledge Spans. Only she possessed this knowledge and she'd come into it purely by accident (or divine intervention) at the young age of 1200 years.

When Jana was a child, she'd once run into the dense forest at one of the highest elevations on her planet. She'd been missing for days and Dakkar was beside himself with Worry. Ashzar had promised her father that he'd search to the ends of the Universe, if it came to that, and he solemnly swore with his life that he'd not return without her. Well......that search was a three month long search. Ashzar had found her in a trance beside a waterway. It was very warm here and it was private. No one else knew of this place. Ashzar had been lead here, though he had no answers as to why, and had been granted access. It was a portal thru which only the "Awakened Ones" or "Special Ones" or the "Ones of Light" could step. She'd discarded her attire earlier and her body still glistened from the sun shining on a moist, wet body from the swim she'd just recently taken.

Funny how, even in her trance, she watched Ashzar as he approached. She was totally at peace, so was not startled by the fact that Uncle Ash had caught her in a complete state of undress. The anger on Ashzar's face faded away as the beauty of the child before him, a golden aura of light completely surrounding her entire being, settled itself somewhere deep within the recesses of his very life's core. He could not describe the emotions within himself; they were not sordid, only peaceful and fulfilling in a way that somehow completed all that he was.

Ashzar had taught Jana to meditate. He'd taught her all types of mind maneuvering and manipulation and he'd taught her to always use it for the good of the Universe. He'd make her practice time and time again. But real wisdom would have to come from her individual experiences. He taught her to seek those experiences. And he'd taught her to not be afraid of the lessons put before her. So he knew not to interfere in this state he found her in. He sat down to wait.

Jana watched him. She smiled inwardly. He was at peace and she could clearly see it, feel it, and that was good to her. She'd come to this place as a result of practicing meditation. She had become anxious as to what Ashzar wanted of her; impatient as to where being in this state was supposed to take her. Her mind had stilled and she heard her name being called softly.

"Ja – Na –a –a……….Ja – Na – a – a……….rise child and follow the sound. Do not be afraid. We are the essence of pure love. Be unafraid; just follow the sound of your name. Ja – Na – a – a …….Ja – Na – a – a ……..

Jana followed the sound and learned from Masters from the dimensions far beyond and above her own. They loved her and taught her and blinded her with light of the knowledge of 1,000's upon 1,000's of Universes. It's the reason she began to acquire and understand knowledge beyond her years. It's the reason Ashzar was in awe of her quantum leap spurts of growth and though he couldn't understand things in their entirety, he grew to love her more each day, each month, each year until he thought he'd go insane holding all this within.

Jana arose, dressed, and then came out of her trance. She walked over to Ashzar, took his hand and innocently said, "We can go now Uncle Ash. How long have I been asleep?" Ashzar simply stated, "Not long Jana. Not long." No words beyond this were ever exchanged around the incident. It was right, somehow.

Jana quickened her pace and headed for Ashzar's Cabin. Why this thought should have come to her as she was being examined, she hadn't a clue, but years ago she'd hidden a piece of crystal shaped crudely like a key with sharp edges in varying lengths surrounding it, in a compartment she'd found in Ashzar's Quarters. Even Ashzar knew nothing of this place. She kicked the bottom lever on the chair at his navigation table. Its vibration would automatically knock open the overhead compartment just up above the table. Grinning at the fact that this small feat charged her somehow, she reached in and grabbed a pair of Ashzar's Visual protectors. Eyes covered, she unscrewed the molecular tubing at the base of the seat of his chair and an object wrapped in a soft black Atominite cloth dropped into her hand. She uncovered the object and activated it to gaze upon its beauty. This was the shut down key to the Lemurian Crystal. To gaze upon it without visual protection while it was activated was to be blinded for eternity, but to touch it was a sure death sentence.

"Ah-kaa-Nee ooh-sha-Nee-sha
Whish-na-ta-na Whish-na-ta-na
Ah-kaa-Nee ooh-sha-Nee-sha
FromtheemaynoharmbedoneOM-M-M-M-mmmm"

The crystal dimmed and became cool to the touch. Jana removed her visor, but placed it in a hook on her belt. She was not sure why she knew these things; she only knew that she did. She also knew she needed to get to the Lemurian Crystal before Ashzar and his crew did. They knew to put visors on, but they did not know not to touch it without shutting it down. Now she understood why Drake always gave excuses as to why she could never board his ship. The missing Crystal had been there all these years once he'd earned the level and clearance to operate a large craft. How he'd gotten access to it was something she'd run over and over in her mind, but she knew for sure he had at one time possessed this key. She'd retrieved it from her small shuttle craft he'd borrowed and then returned in some great hurry, not having time to talk to her at all on that particular day. For some unknown reason, she'd searched her craft and found the key. He'd never been sure exactly where he might have left it. She'd known, somehow, back then how to shut down the power of the key. And she'd sensed it was important to Drake, judging how irate he was upon misplacing it. So she'd hidden it in Ashzar's Chair and promptly forgot about it. So............Drake Traitor had access to the Lemurian Crystal and the key. He'd known how to shut it down, but how? What really mattered was that he had shut it down long enough to have gotten it on his ship on a platform, reenergized it once it was in place, then lost the key. Oh – this was dangerous, this was very dangerous and she knew the fate of the entire crew rested upon her shoulders.

Jana sat down wearily. She knew what she had to do. Ashzar must know of this. He "had" to listen to her. She'd give it one last possible try. Switching on the communication system, she tapped the icon that connected her to the private officers' quarters. "High Commander Ashzar, I offer a truce and I implore you to hear the information I have to give concerning your mission to overcome the Dark Forces. I am in your Quarters; please.....sit in counsel with me. Ignoring my request could result in the death of your crew and the weight of this would fall squarely on your shoulders for failing that of which you've been so magnificently gifted to command." Softly she spoke, not realizing her next words were being heard....... "Please Ash, don't shut me out. I love you."

Jana slouched in her chair and bawled her heart out, unaware she'd forgotten to kill the icon and Ashzar was hearing every wretched, agonizing sob. She'd just sacrificed herself for the sake of her people. Her life and career as she'd always known it to be was suddenly at its end.

CHAPTER 20
REFLECTIONS

Ashzar quickly reassessed all the available data as Jana left the Command Bridge. Navigation had just finished plotting all the necessary star-field data and position vectors into the main computer and he made a mental note to review the programming before they actually needed it to save themselves. It was very crowded on the Command Bridge, yet eerily quiet. Even with a double crew on duty, everyone had more to accomplish in a short time than was normally remotely possible.

Ashzar had been planning on the run. He had no concrete plan for obtaining the crystal. Assuming he was able to acquire the crystal, he was not sure his escape plan would work. In fact, the only thing he was really sure of was that something was wrong, he could not directly sense what it might be and he continued to draw up and discard segments of a plan hoping his sense of something wrong would change.

Drake Traitor was incensed that his plans had not followed their prescribed course and reached their desired conclusion. No matter, he was so confident in the power he possessed through the Lemurian Crystal that he was not really concerned with minor details that happened along the way. It was a lifetime's work of deception and fraud that enabled him to obtain the crystal in the first place.

Traitor had learned early in life that all sentient beings were equal in the eyes of the Universe. However, the reality of the situation seemed to always favor those who took advantage of a situation.

It seemed that the lesson the Universe taught over and over again was that nice guys finish last. There were long periods of time when he strived to be like his friend Ashzar and follow an enlightened path. He had in this lifetime been responsible for saving entire worlds from paths of self-destruction. He was very skilled in many arts and sciences and was painfully aware of all the shortcomings of both. Now as he sat in the crystal chamber and pondered how to finish that fool Ashzar and possess that pesky Jana for himself, he realized that power was what he had been seeking all along and it was time he used his for his own gain. The Universe owed him.

Drake Traitor began ordering his crew to position his ship so that he could more closely monitor the Command Ship and the Free Spirit. He smiled as he wondered if Ashzar realized that he was powerless to stop this destruction. Traitor decided a nice game of cat and mouse would deflect his attention from dwelling too long on his memories of Jana chained to the pole at the Crystal Post. Such a spell she wove for him, her magic reached deep into his soul and he burned with a desire and lust to possess her, not just physically, but at every level. He closed his eyes and floated gently on the sea of his mind as he saw the possession of that wretched woman take many forms. Oh well, only a little longer and she would cease to exist as Jana, Daughter of Dakkar and would become Jana, slave to Traitor the Great!

Ashzar was aware that his own assessment of the situation was not entirely correct. Drake Traitor was not attacking them yet on any level and he had imagined at least some kind of attack before now. He knew that as long as Traitor used conventional weapons, the Command Ship and the Free Spirit were safe within the shields of the Command Ship. It occurred to Ashzar that Traitor might not have mastered the powers of the crystal and was unable to do more than a few parlor tricks. However, he knew that he was unwilling to risk so many lives to find out and so time was his greatest resource and he probed and poked into every tiny bit of information looking for a way to gain an advantage. Still, that voice in his head would not stop reminding him that something was wrong; he just could not focus on its cause.

A part of Ashzar's mind followed the uneasiness into the recesses of his knowledge and began looking for the cause. Ordinarily, Ashzar would have completely ignored such a little nagging thought, but this one would not go away and it was necessary to give it some ground. Suddenly, he knew that Jana was the key to his doubts. As he began looking back at what she had done to trigger such doubt in him, her voice rang out in his ear, startling him to full alertness.

As he listened to her message with his full attention, it was clear that she was very disturbed and emotional. He listened and immediately began weighing her words. When it seemed she had finished, he was deciding how to address her when those final words echoed softly in his ears. Ashzar had always loved the lore that grew up around Cupid, one of the lesser Masters who visited many worlds and spread love. Right now he would have preferred to never have heard of Cupid as Jana's words triggered emotions and memories that were buried so deep inside that he shuddered and gasped at their strength. As the memories of other planes of understanding and a soul level emotion poured out, he knew and saw that his relationship with Jana would never be the same again.

Ashzar found that even with the weight of the crisis situation firmly resting on his shoulders, he was nervous as he awaited Jana's appearance for the second time in the private officers' quarters where he had summoned her following her message. Pandora's proverbial Box was flung wide open and he and Jana were caught holding the lid.

Upon receiving Jana's request to grant her counsel time, Ashzar's mind immediately rejected the request, thinking about times past when Jana's words usually ended as a sword entering into his heart and sliding straight out through his back. She usually had an ulterior motive for her carefully laid out words or actions; some hidden agenda always just beneath the surface of that of which was actually presented to him. She was cunning enough to always come out the victor and, Dammit!, he didn't have the time to fence with her now. But then the next words she spoke caused emotions to boil to the surface that Ashzar could not put reigns on.

Something was different in the sound of her voice. A sadness, perhaps a heaviness, perhaps even a surrender of sorts came thru to him and he simply could not ignore the vibrations the sound emitted within his emotional sensory fields. Her sobs were of an unusual high frequency sonic vibration and it tore at him like no laser beam ever could. He could never feel totally at ease with her. It was as if she could see into his mind and read all his thoughts. As if......??? Her powers of the mind were so closely matched to his own that the woman actually scared him at times. She forced him to use an over-load of energy, just keeping mental blocks in place, to be sure he kept certain information out of her mental scope range.

Sure – he had taught her to use her mind in this way and had "forced" her to practice each and every day. Sometimes 2 and 3 times a day. She'd resented him at the time, but he'd wanted her to have every power available to her in times of emergency or great need. After a time though, the only way Jana could cope with these sessions was to make a game of them. Hell! She made a game of everything until she became so good at the games she played.....she could pick up thought probes or thought transmissions, Negative or Positive, without even intending to. She could split her higher self into two parts. One picked up thoughts and stored them for future assessment, while the other led a seemingly normal interaction with whoever was before her in the instant.

Ashzar hit his head with the heel of the palm of his hand as if to rid himself of unwanted thoughts and said, "Commander, I will speak with you here in the Private Officers Quarters. I must demand that this conversation be short as time is not on our side. So make haste Commander. I will await your presence."

Jana wasted no time in returning to the Officers Quarters. It was imperative that Ashzar be made privy to the information she held. The lives of her people and of the man she loved depended upon it. Though she knew the mission could not be accomplished without her, she felt no elation that Ashzar would be forced to succumb to her wishes. His main concern was to keep her safe at all cost and she was actually sorry for the fact that her importance to him was a worry that he could do without, during this coming confrontation with Drake Traitor.

Jana summoned permission to enter thru the Voice Activation System. Stepping thru the entryway, Jana locked eyes with Ashzar. "Sit Commander. What is this matter of urgency you wish to inform me of that you feel I don't already have access to?" Ashzar cocked a brow at Jana and she took a deep breath to control the immediate an-ger the man always seemed to be able to invoke upon her person.

"High Commander, Sir," Jana began. "Drake Traitor sits upon a power of which there is no possible way for you to compete – without knowledge of the very power you are competing against. Commander, could you please reiterate for me exactly what it is you and your crew think you are up against and how you intend to accomplish the goals you have set in place?"

Ashzar sighed with more than a little disgust and his voice was quite harsh as he said, "Commander it is not a requirement to reiterate anything to you if I do not wish to do so and my decision is not to do so. And why do you have those ridiculous Visual Protectors on your person? Do you not think me intelligent enough to know that visual protection is what's needed in connection with being in the vicinity of the Lemurian Crystal?" Ashzar smiled a mocking smile which incensed Jana's anger to the boiling point.

"I beg your pardon, Sir," Jana spoke each word distinctly, dripping with sarcasm and venom. "If that was stated by my person as an implication against your vast knowledge and intelligence, then please accept my apology. As to the reason for the Visual Protectors I carry.....I will demonstrate my purposes shortly. It is not my intention to waste your time or to compete with your wisdom. It is my intention, however Sir, to be of service to you and present every available minute piece of knowledge within my "humble" arena scope of information to assure the safety of you, your crew AND the people of the Pleiadian sector."

Jana proceeded to give full account of the workings of Drake Traitor when they were siblings up to and including the point of how she came into possession of the key, where it was hidden and her puzzlement of her knowledge of how to turn it on and shut it off. She then handed each officer a pair of the visual protectors and demonstrated the truth of what she spoke. She ended her case with, "So now, High Commander, perhaps you can see that I need to be a part of this mission whether I am welcomed or not. For some odd reason I think there are three of us with the knowledge or at least the gift of the machinations of the key. I believe those three persons to be Drake Traitor, of course, myself and YOU......High Commander.

Ashzar had turned Ashen, a stricken look on his face. Jana continued, "It is only a very strong feeling I have on this and wish to test my theory now. It is my belief that a higher Power from realms beyond our own has a hand in this. It is the only explanation that makes any sense to me." Jana handed Ashzar a piece of Metallic looking parchment with the Activation incantation on it.

"FromtheemaynoharmbedoneOM-M-M-M-mmmm
Ah-Kaa-Nee ooh-sha-Knee-sha
Whish-na-ta-na Whish-na-ta-na
Ah-Kaa-Nee ooh-sha-Nee-sha"

"Please place this in your memory scope to see if it triggers feelings of familiarity, then swallow the parchment. It is sacred. I also know that the key is in the possession of its rightful handler. That handler is me, High Commander. For whatever reason I have no clue. But I do know that this key must be inserted into the crystal at a specific angle and must only touch certain portions of the crystal going into it. The slightest error would cause disaster. I don't understand the whole purpose of the number three, only that it constitutes balance in some way. I can only theorize once again and that hypothesis is this..........

< In the beginning the number 3 was good, one fell to ruin
And the power of that one was so great – it would take the
Power of the remaining 2, together, to be able to hold the
Now evil one at bay and to bring that which is in error back
Into balance.>"

Jana paused for effect before beginning again. "One factual source of power we have to our advantage is that Drake Traitor does not think clearly when he is highly agitated and angry. There is no greater source of anger where Drake Traitor is concerned than when you are in his presence, High Commander. Only you know the reasons for this sir. I won't even attempt the pretense of such knowledge. I do, however, have a suggestion to put before you sir and make no mistake.....it is only a suggestion, not an attempt to force your hand in any way."

Jana paused again to collect her thoughts and then continued. "Before I make the suggestion, I must first know if my 1st theory is correct. I have activated the key to the crystal as you have all witnessed. This special Metallic material allows me to handle it while it is activated. High Commander, Sir!! Please shut it down if you can........."

Ashzar stared at Jana as if she'd gone absolutely insane, but he closed his eyes and shut out all distraction and concentrated only to humor her and then perhaps when he could not do this impossible thing she imagined, she'd see that what she really needed was a long, long, convalescence period, but, to his utter astonishment he began to intone in a whisper that only Jana could hear with her gift of Long Range Audio Reception....

"Ah-kaa-Nee ooh-sha-Nee-sha
Whish-na-ta-na Whish-na-ta-na
Ah-kaa-Nee ooh-sha-Nee-sha
FromtheemaynoharmbedoneOM-M-M-M-mmmm"

The crystal shut down and Ashzar could only stare at Jana and say........ "What is this suggestion, Commander?"

Jana smiled and spoke softly. "Very good Commander. The shut down atonement is the reverse of the activation atonement. Sir, if you could distract Drake Traitor with a conversation that is a sore spot between the two of you, I could use a power I have – that I have never spoken of to you. I will admit I truly do not wish to do so now because it is a power which gave me an advantage many times, but for the sake of my people, I have no choice but to make the sacrifice. Commander....I can make myself become invisible in much the same way we make our ships become invisible. Normally, I need no assistance in obtaining this state, however, as you've stated quite correctly, I am not physically 100% in top shape........" Jana's voice trailed off. "Sir, I need you to split your energies like you do when you commit part of your energies to the problems of Earth, but at the same time use the remaining energy to command your star fleets. I am soliciting a portion of your energy while at the same time you distract Drake Traitor. I can slip in and de-activate the crystal with this key leaving it available to be moved by means of whatever tactics you have previously laid plans to. The key will remain on my person and I will replace it in its ancient resting place. There is only one cause for concern that I can think of. Drake Traitor is also a "sensitive" such as ourselves, Commander. He may be able to pick up on my molecular residue. If he's kept busy enough, however, we just may be able to pull this thing off." She looked at Ashzar, sparkles once again in her eyes and asked, "What do you say Commander. Is this suggestion feasible...................?"

Ashzar knew that Jana was right. It took about a millisecond for him to assess his feelings and merge them with the facts as he now understood them and make a judgment. "We have much planning to do for this mission and even then, we have to get out of this space and back to our own. I will strongly consider your presentation, Commander, and keep you informed. Will you join us for the remainder of this meeting?" The veteran officer nudged the newest Officer who had questioned Commander Ashzar's disciplinary tactics and said, "See? What did I tell you?" The new officer smiled and said, "Yeah, I'm beginning to understand now. Thanks for the heads-up advice. I won't forget it going forward."

Details were tried and discarded, new tactics described, evaluated and suggested and the group continued working toward a plan with a reasonable success probability. Neural Network computers ran simulation right on the wall screen. As was expected, none of the scenarios favored the Forces of Dakkar or the Superior Council of the Pleiades.

Ashzar felt it first, a barely perceptible shift in the energies around them. As alarms began sounding throughout the Command Ship, it was the face of Drake Traitor that appeared on all the view-screens and view-walls. Every member of the crew watched as his face twisted into a grotesque snarl and he hissed, "Ashzar, I tire of sitting here watching for you to try and escape. You always were a little scared of me, I knew that all along. Usually, I let you beat me just because I wanted you to accept me as a friend. Well, no more! You have something I want besides your petty little life and I think it is time for me to collect. I make a final offer; send Jana, that spoiled brat over to my ship now and you follow in a few hours and I will let everyone else go free. Of course, only I have the power to send them back to our Universe. You hear me Ashzar?"

Amazingly enough, his face twisted into an even more sinister snarl. "I know you hear me assmunch and I know your whole ship can hear me. I have always known that you hid behind the power of Dakkar and were a coward at heart. Answer me you, you, you.....well, whatever you are. I am pure power now, you see, and I have control. You are not going to live to see another planet saved or even another meal."

The hatred on Drake Traitor's face seemed to dissolve into a look of amusement. He continued to leer at the crew from every monitor, but his attention seemed to be elsewhere. Ashzar was frantically working with the communications to try and block the intrusion into his systems. He seemed to be every place on the ship at once, encouraging, sensing, aiding, and helping. All the while, the face of his nemesis was still on every viewer on the ship and nothing seemed to be able to change that fact.

The shuttle bay was abuzz with talk of the upcoming mission and Drake Traitor's ability to override the Command Ship's communications systems. All aboard knew that they had the best equipment available to the Federation of Planets and not one of them had ever seen a failure like this one. Already there were whispers about the valor of their Commander when Ashzar arrived suddenly to check mission progress.

"Sir," intoned a crew member named Vasgitz, "all preparations are proceeding according to instructions and we will be ready in a few minutes."

An unaccustomed mumble was the best Ashzar could manage as he methodically surveyed the area and double checked some supply rosters. "Very well, Vasgitz, continue. I shall continue to prepare and will expect to hear from you soon."

CHAPTER 21
HUMILIATION AND CAPTURE

Ashzar paused briefly as he surveyed the faces of each member. "I think it is much too impetuous and dangerous for you to risk your life this way, however, I will concede that I can think of no other way to extricate ourselves from this mess. It is imperative that Drake Traitor not be allowed to unleash the power of that crystal on peaceful beings in our own Universe or any Universe for that matter. It must end here or we must perish trying to stop it."

Jana saw the loss in his eyes and her heart reached out to him in a way he alone could feel. She knew that now more than ever in her long life that she needed him and his wisdom and she also knew that this state of despair restricted him severely. "Let's assemble back in the officers' quarters and continue developing our plan," was all she could think of to say at the moment, surprised at her loss for words.

The entire bridge crew had been sitting silently for the few minutes since Drake Traitor's communication had started. Now Ashzar went to each crew member at their positions and quietly said a few words to each. With a final look around the familiar faces, he bowed slightly, turned and left the bridge.

"You all know what must be done, and I know it will be done. I thank you all and love you all." Jana immediately realized the lump in her throat prevented any further words, so she followed Ashzar from the bridge.

Chaos was the only way to describe the scene in the officers' conference room when Jana entered. Everyone seemed to be talking at once and no one seemed to be listening to anything. Jana made her way around the room and took her usual seat beside Ashzar. He was in a heated discussion with his Supply Commander, a handsome male from Orion. Something about having room for everyone to suit up prior to the attack. She could hear similar arguments and disagreements from all over the room, and none of them were helping, this she knew. She closed her eyes and transported herself mentally to a place where a beautiful city of every imaginable hue rose from the bottom of the sea. Jana was aware of her surroundings on board the Command Ship and would have responded had anyone directed conversation her way, but her awareness was centered in the underwater paradise spread around her consciousness.

She could not explain this exactly, but she knew this place and visited whenever she needed peace and calmness restored. As she drifted above the splendid city below her, a lone swimmer seemed to notice her and swam upward from a large ornate structure. The sunlight filtering down from the surface lent a surreal effect to the place, but Jana knew in her heart that this was as real as the ship where her body was aware of the ongoing arguments and conversations.

As the swimmer came close, Jana was aware of the melodic music that seemed to come from everywhere. She and the swimmer merged in an embrace that caused them to swirl around like an underwater ballet. "Garth!" she exclaimed. "I am so glad to see you again," as she allowed the slow dance and hug to continue a long moment. Jana's lithe form seemed to merge with the muscular body of the swimmer and they slowly released their grips and looked at each other while still holding each other close.

"Jana, Wami and I have been following the ebb and flow of the energy in the Universe and we are aware that a critical junction has occurred in the continuum. I was sure you were involved because I could sense an undertone of you in the energy. I hope you can explain what is happening and what disturbs the fabric of our time and space."

"Garth my old friend, it is such a frightful and lengthy tale, I would share it if only there was time. Yes, the Universe is threatened. We are going to remove that threat very soon. I came to visit only briefly to restore my sanity and to gather strength for the coming storm." As Jana spoke, she and Garth were slowly drifting down toward the City of Aquarius or better known as "Mystic City." Jana had been able to visit this underwater world for as long as she could remember. She also knew that she had visited here and lived here in other time-places and that her soul was a fragment of, or a connection to, many of the beings who dwelled here now.

Others were gathering around Jana and Garth now, and excited chatter was quickly spreading through the city. Telepathic communication certainly had the advantage of speed. A respectful distance separated Jana and Garth from the other swimmers as they reached a wide avenue running off toward the city's center.

"Garth, even with the time differential between this world and mine, I must only be here a moment. You have my eternal gratitude for that warm greeting and for restoring some of my spirit. You always know what I need and I love you."

Garth looked around at the beautiful city for a moment and softly took Jana's hand and led her inside the large hall in front of them. Once inside the bejeweled entryway, he said, "wait here, I will return in an instant." Without waiting, he disappeared around a corner and was gone. She relaxed and let a tendril of her awareness drift toward the Command Ship. The time there was very slow relative to this underwater world and she was happy to note that the raging storm in the conference room had not abated. She could stay a while longer.

"Jana," Garth called as he came around the corner and startled her. Even a mental shout could startle if it was loud. "I am painfully aware of your limited time, but I have something to give you before you go back." He unfolded his hand and in it was the most perfect black pearl that Jana had ever imagined. "This jewel has served us well in the past and now it will serve you well as you complete the task ahead of you."

Jana knew better than to argue with Garth so she accepted the lustrous orb from him and as she gazed at it, she realized it had a light and energy all its own. "Garth and people of Aquarius, I Jana, Daughter of Dakkar, accept this gift and swear an oath to you to use it well and allow its beauty to touch my soul. Before such a gift given with pure love, I am insignificant and pale in its light."

Applause and laughter arose on all sides as she slipped the pearl inside her tunic of the two-piece jumpsuit. Without further words,

Jana slowly swam out of the entryway and began heading toward the surface. As she glanced down, she could see hundreds of inhabitants of Aquarius looking up at her and she could feel their energy and almost hear her name as love flowed all around her.

"Jana!" The shout brought her abruptly back into the conference room aboard the Command Ship. She opened her eyes and saw that several people were looking at her as if expecting an answer. "I'm sorry. I must have drifted off a moment."

"Do you need any support from the quartermaster to accomplish your mission?" a young officer shouted over the noise of the other conversations in the room. "Ah, no, thanks, I don't think so," she mumbled. She put her hand into her space jump suit pocket and was not surprised to feel the warmth and smoothness of something spherical. "Thank you again Garth," she thought as a smile passed briefly over her face. She returned to the planning session with renewed vigor and a confidence that all would be well now. Before she knew it, Jana was hurrying through the Command Ship toward the shuttle bay and perhaps the most important mission of this crew's life was beginning.

The approach to Drake Traitor's ship was quiet. Jana closed her eyes and had time to think back to the beginning of this adventure and reflected that there was only one real reason that she and Ashzar were here at all to defend the known Universes from this incarnate evil. For a long time, she had wondered if life had a partner capable of a life with her. Not only capable, but worthy. She decided it was her right to search for a life partner that was a match for her. Oh sure, there were plenty of good men, and women too, (as the soul within a body is androgynous), that would love to be the companion of someone so high in the hierarchy of the affairs of Man, but she wanted THE ONE. Her face twisted into an expression that was at the time a smile and a painful grimace. They were here because she knew at the core of her being that whatever she tried to tell herself, her soul was linked to Ashzar and she would settle for no less. She knew the man inside and out. Knew that he would pursue her and bring her back if at all possible. It was this probability of spending time with him in deep space that started this whole adventure. She opened her eyes and looked across the cargo bay of the shuttle and saw that the hand-picked crew members were already putting on their skin-suits for the coming attack.

A skin suit was one of the gifts presented to the Universe by an ancient and obscure race living on the fringe of the galaxy. The ulnpt technology was entirely organic and it was still a shock to view one of their huge organic Freeships in orbit around a planet. Looking more like an array of disheveled tree trunks, these massive semi-sentient structures could grow new parts as needed by their space-faring creators.

The skin suit was no less a marvel. All the user had to do was place a small rubbery "nut" on their heads and wait for the suit to sense their body heat. The suit would slowly begin to glow with a soft, golden light and flow down the wearer's head, much like an egg squashed on the head. As it flowed down toward the wearer's feet, it coated the entire body with a tough, resilient, translucent sheath. Normal bodily functions were still possible as the covering seemed to sense the needs of the wearer. Sweat was carried away from the skin of the suit, as the suit sealed itself tightly, and generated a heat of its own depending on the wearer's needs. In a normal environment, it would allow normal respiration and always made the wearer comfortable. In severe conditions, such as space, it sealed itself tightly and was able to somehow provide the wearer with oxygen and heat for up to an hour. Longer periods of time seemed to deplete the resources of the skin-suit and the thing simply thinned out and vanished.

Even in the hectic rush to be ready for this mission, Jana could not help but admire the strategy being used. The skin-suits would allow debarkation to several of Ashzar's troops so that they could complete their part of the mission outside in space without any metal or electrical components to give them away to Drake Traitor's sensors.

As the shuttle made its final approach, Jana was startled to hear Drake Traitor's voice on the intercom channel. It seems he and Ashzar were having an ongoing conversation as Drake could not resist baiting his prey. Ashzar was playing his part well and even the vilest of taunts from Drake about what he was going to do to Jana while Ashzar watched had no effect on him. In fact, it was evident that Drake Traitor was getting more agitated by the minute as the two of them traded insults back and forth. Some of the words Ashzar used caused her to wonder just how many space bars the man had visited. Finally, all plans had been polished, all troops were in place as much as possible and the shuttle docked in the shuttle landing bay of Drake Traitor's ship.

As the door opened, Drake Traitor's voice was coming from the shuttle landing bay. "Welcome aboard. I cannot believe how easy this has been. Please do not invoke my anger further by attempting something as stupid as bringing a weapon with you. Follow the red arrows that appear on the floor in front of you and do not stop if you value your life at all. Ha – ha – ha – ha – ha....." His laughter was enough to almost break Jana's resolve to be strong.

Ashzar and Jana began slowly walking along the shuttle bay floor and followed the bright red arrows that kept appearing some few feet ahead of them. They entered a hallway and as it turned and twisted through the bowels of the ship, they were aware that their progress was being observed by crew members stationed along the way in cubbies or side hallways. They arrived at a lift and followed the arrows inside. The doors closed and the lift whisked them away toward whatever Drake Traitor planned as a reception.

The lift doors opened directly onto the command bridge of Traitor's ship. Visors were handed to Ashzar and Jana by one of his troops. He was seated across the space from them and several heavily armed troops surrounded him. Off to the left, the Lemurian Crystal gave off a brilliant glow, but their attention was on the person ignoring the new arrivals. They slowly walked across the Command Bridge toward him and he looked up and shouted, "Stop! It is not every day that I have such distinguished visitors aboard my ship and I want to make this victory as sweet as possible. Daughter of Drakkar, come forward and present yourself properly to me. Not you, Ashwipe. You will get your turn when I have decided exactly how to humiliate you most."

Jana felt a chill run down her spine as the attentions of the evil Dark lord focused on her. She slowly took a step in his direction and sensed that Ashzar moved along with her. He stopped when commanded to do so by Drake Traitor and she slowly made her way toward the area where he stood with his troops.

Drake was enjoying the moment more than anything he could remember in his long and colorful life. He knew that it was his right to have this kind of power, but he had never experienced such satisfaction from the thought of merely possessing a female. It was a fate far worse than possession that he had planned for her, but only after he had exhausted ways to torment her and that cursed Ashzar. As she drew closer to him, he could not help smiling as waves of ecstasy washed though his body and mind. "Close enough for now wench!" he fairly shouted. "Stand right there and pay close attention."

Jana stopped and watch in horror as Drake Traitor stretched forth his hands and pointed toward Ashzar. A luminous wave seemed to flow from the massive crystal toward Traitor's outstretched hands and concentrate before flowing straight toward Ashzar. The glow engulfed him entirely although Jana could still see him plainly inside the corona forming around him. Ashzar's body was jerking and twisting as the energy wave seared every muscle and membrane in his body.

"Walk!" screamed Traitor as Ashzar slowly took a step in his direction. "Come closer to me and feel the wrath of one you have never had the common sense to respect. How does it feel to be in my complete control? How many ways can you imagine dying Ashzar? How much pain can you absorb before you cease to exist?" Drake Traitor was grinning like one possessed as Ashzar slowly put one foot in front of the other and moved straight toward the monster controlling him. Ever so slowly Ashzar moved across the bridge. It was obvious to Jana that he was using all of his power to control himself and not give Traitor the satisfaction of knowing the immense pain created by the constant flow of energy. His muscles were not his to command, his senses were nearly useless as his body dealt with the searing white-hot pain in every fiber of his being. He at once discovered that if he did not resist as much, the pain eased slightly. Before he could explore the technique further, Drake Traitor ordered him to stop.

"Fall down on your face and bow at the feet of your conqueror, dog." Ashzar's body was visibly turning into a mass of knotted muscle as he felt the weight of the Universe pushing him down to the floor. Jana's sanity threatened to flee as she yelled out, "Stop this madness Drake! For the love of the Universe! Are you truly this vile? I have grown up loving you like a brother. No one could have made me believe that you had grown so evil if I hadn't witnessed it with my own eyes. Is the hatred inside of you so consuming and your heart so infectiously cancerous that it has caused you to lose sight of the light? What happened to the Drake Traitor I use to know?"

"Silence!" Traitor looked at Jana with eyes that looked like slivers of Glass and spoke in a voice that warranted no debating. "Not one more word unless I tell you to speak! Move and you'll wish you'd never been born. How dare you even begin to think that you and I have ever been on the same level. You will always be beneath me, you spoiled space brat. I suggest you save your energy. You're going to need all you've got!"

As Traitor berated Jana, Ashzar got the opportunity to stop fighting the force. It eased and allowed him to almost control his fall into a prone position in front of the Dark lord. Several of Traitor's troops, following some prearranged or unspoken order, formed a line between Where Ashzar lay face down on the deck and the still grinning Dark Lord. Ashzar's body began writhing like a snake and moving through the isle of troops toward Traitor's position. He was struggling again to maintain some control, but it was obviously more than he was capable of doing. "Coward," a small voice croaked from Ashzar and he twisted into a ball of pure pain from the effort.

"It is easy to call me names and vent your anger on me. Struggle you worm and crawl a little faster please. You are beginning to be a bore." Traitor assumed a faint amused look as he continued to pump energy from the crystal to the man wallowing on the floor in front of him. "Before this day is over, you and that snot-nosed tramp that came with you are going to begin to experience pain on a level you have not *ever* imagined. I can't believe how easily I was able to pull off this little plan and grant myself the pleasures you afford me now."

Ashzar had stopped crawling again and was only a few feet in front of Drake Traitor. No sound came from Ashzar as he used his mental capacity to call upon his body and spirit to provide the strength he must have to save any of them.

Jana watched in horror as the energy field visibly beat Ashzar down to the floor and made his body crawl in a manner that made her sick to watch. As he continued to slowly crawl across the floor, the odor of sweat and the fear she felt, made her double over clearly nauseated. Traitor quickly glanced at her, but immediately returned his concentration to Ashzar. With the energy field holding him in place, there seemed to be nothing Ashzar could do to resist the Dark lord.

Ashzar found that he had no control of his body. Getting one word out of his throat had cost him dearly in reserve strength. He knew in order for the plan to have any chance at success, he had to be a major distraction, but he could not resist the raw energy pouring over him. As he came to the feet of his tormentor, he was held motionless as Traitor rested his foot on Ashzar's head. "Now who has the power old friend? Who controls the largest power source in the known Universe? Who is going to finally beat you?"

The thought of being the single most powerful person in the Universe was like a powerful drug to Traitor. He had a twisted smile on his face again and was muttering to himself. As he basked in the knowledge of the destruction all this power could do for him, he relaxed his grip on Ashzar who responded by immediately whispering, "You....are not.....capable....of ....beating ....Me." The effort caused him to collapse and writhe in pain once more. The energy flow visibly lessened and Drake Traitor removed his foot from his head.

"This is as close to pure pleasure as I can imagine. I suppose you are good for something after all." Drake Traitor spat on Ashzar as he continued, "You and I go back a long time and you more than anyone should understand that a genius like myself could not live in the shadow of others. Perhaps I could let you live as my puppet and you could see what changes I am going to bring to the so called enlightened races."

Ashzar was aware that the power holding him had lessened and so he tried to talk again. "I will die before I would ever serve you in any capacity."

"Ashzar my dear fool, I have power that even you cannot fight. Watch this." He looked over to where Jana was standing and as his gaze fell on her, the energy flow split and part of it now flowed around her, engulfing her in the same aura as Ashzar.

"Kneel, Woman, and prepare to do my bidding." Jana felt herself lose her will and her body fell to its knees on the floor. She decided not to attempt to resist until she learned more about what was happening.

"Let's see if Ashzar can stand the sight of seeing you in excruciating pain, knowing he's powerless to stop it! Beg me to end the life of that Bastard and I just may show you a little leniency." Traitor said with the smile returning to his face. He directed more of the searing, hot energy toward her; energy that was so hot it melted the cosmic thread of her garment and it feel to the floor. Jana screamed for mercy! Tears rolled down her face as she realized that the power commanded by this monster was more than she could ever resist. As she struggled and fought against the forces ruling her body, she knew she had lost this round and was soon begging Traitor to end the life of the only man she had ever truly loved. At that moment Traitor was the one person, in her lifespan, she had allowed herself to truly hate. Hate was not a part of her make-up and she didn't like the feeling.

Drake Traitor was by no means distracted by her anguish and continued to keep Ashzar immobile on the floor while he thought of the many ways to degrade her. He had no intention of showing either of them any mercy. Wracked with intense pain, Jana was quickly beginning to lose her mental capacity. Ashzar could not turn his head or close his eyes and was forced to watch the degradation of the woman he loved.

The human body is capable of many things given sufficient stimulation. With every bit of strength he could manage from within and without, Ashzar moved his hand a millimeter at a time and was able to grab Drake Traitor's ankle. Immediately Traitor's other foot came up and stomped the hand extended to his ankle. "You dare to touch the Lord of the Universe, you worm? Perhaps we need another diversion to entertain us!" A huge hand seemed to shove Ashzar across the floor to the feet of the guards.

Jana watched in horror as the proud and fierce Ashzar was about to be attacked by this group of deviants. Traitor was getting more excited by the minute and was now visibly shaking with excitement as he walked over to get a closer look at Ashzar's plight. Suddenly, Traitor tilted his head back and closed his eyes to savor the victory he was so sure was within his power. The energy field locking Jana in place slackened noticeably and she found she had some movement. Without pause, she retrieved the key from what used to be her garment and began to slowly move toward the crystal and Traitor's source of power.

Jana could not fathom where she got the strength, but she aimed the key precisely toward the space in the still glowing Lemurian Crystal. Suddenly, it was as if every pain she had ever experienced came at once. She was absolutely blind in the white hot heat of pure pain. A vision of Drake Traitor was all she could see as his power diverted itself from Ashzar and focused on stopping her from covering the few feet to the crystal. She could not bear the pain, but it was small compared to the loss she felt at failing in her mission. As consciousness began to leave her pain wracked body, her final thought was "Forgive me my love, I have failed."

Ashzar was faintly aware of what was happening to him as he lay powerless on the floor. The voice inside screamed at him to distract Drake Traitor somehow and with all the will he could summon, he managed to move his hand enough to touch Traitor's ankle. The effect was immediate. All of the Dark lord's power focused on him and he lost all touch with the reality he was experiencing.

After a few seconds in the wastelands of pain, Ashzar was able to discern that something had shifted. As he opened his eyes, he saw Drake Traitor standing looking down at him with a smile on his face. His perspective had changed and now he was partly across the room and surrounded by guards. He could sense that Jana was near and as he focused his eyes on her, he could not hide his disbelief as she began moving toward the Lemurian Crystal. He hadn't been in the position before to witness her first attempt. The key was in her outstretched hand and she was closing ground. As he watched, Ashzar could not help think that she was never going to make it because he knew that the Dark lord's power was focused on her now seemingly frail body.

Jana used every ounce of strength left, to render her body invisible. As Ashzar enjoyed a brief second of no pain, he realized her intentions and added his energies to hers to help fortify the effort. Drake Traitor was confused for only a few seconds, but it was long enough for Jana to get to the crystal and in a slow motion dreamlike movement, the key slid into the ancient space on the artifact.

Instantly, several things happened at once. A roar came from Drake Traitor as the light from the Crystal instantly died. Ashzar bounded from the floor as if shot from a cannon and Jana collapsed onto the deck, visors falling from her face and her invisibility gone from over exertion of painfully delivering the needed energy.

Ashzar, throwing his visors across the room, rushed to the still form of Jana just as the first of his troops bounded into the room. Their report was as expected; no followers of the Dark lord would interrupt them now. Ashzar hardly heard them as he knelt beside the still body of Jana. He picked her head up from the deck and gently began to massage the top while he quietly chanted a short healing song over and over.

"Oh Universes and Worlds of Love and Light,
Healing powers shall this wrong right.
Flow through me with powers bright
And heal this one within your might."

Jana stirred in Ashzar's arms and opened her eyes. "Have we lost our life-force?" were the first words she could say.

Ashzar seemed to start at these words, but laughed out loud and he proclaimed, "No, but I am beginning to think I know the way there and it is a path we must take together, Jana, Princess of Light and Daughter of Dakkar."

After he assured himself that she was in no distress, he gently helped her to her feet and guided her to a seat, handing her the top portion of his space suit to provide her some sort of temporary covering. Ashzar turned to Lord Traitor, who was seated with his head in his hands between two of Ashzar's crew, and said, "Many years have we been opponents in a battle that was never admitted on either side. This episode today is a fortunate one in that no lives were sacrificed needlessly and we may well all live to see the morrow. In my heart, I could never have imagined that the power of the dark forces could affect one as strong as yourself. It is no dishonor to succumb to such a power, and today honor must be carefully weighed as decisions made here will flow outward and have repercussions for generations to come."

"Lord Traitor, as Commander of the Confederation of Light Forces in this sector, I order you and your crew returned to the High Counsel. Greater wisdom will prevail and you will be judged and sentenced fairly. I pledge my honor that it will be so."

Drake Traitor regarded Ashzar with an icy stare as he rose to his feet. "Ashzar, you may think that you have won a great battle today.

I have no choice but to submit to your commands, but do not forget, lo, etch it in your heart where it will never be forgotten.........I shall return in victory and it will be you who stands humbly in defeat."

Sadness seemed to flow over Ashzar as he watched Drake Traitor from across the room. Ashzar was quiet for a moment. Just as he began to move around the huge Lemurian Crystal, his communicator beeped. The voice in his ear told of a Priority One message from one of his captains in orbit around Earth.

"Commander, forgive this intrusion, but the matter is most urgent and requires your immediate attention." Ashzar knew upon hearing the words that contact with Earth must have somehow been established and that the situation must indeed be dire.

Jana was too tired and too weak to try to tune into the communication with Ashzar and whoever he was in counsel with at the moment. Things had somehow turned out successfully for herself and Ashzar and their crew, though she wasn't quite sure how, but she could see that some urgency was in progress by the heightened energy she automatically picked up from watching Ashzar. Her clothes were in tatters on the floor and what she wanted to do most, just now, was to shower and seek her bed and let all emotion just drain from her being. Too many feelings were pouring from her psyche and her heart, and it all threatened to take her to some unknown place she felt she'd rather not be. These thoughts were pushed from her mind, however, as Ashzar moved quickly before her. His eyes softened as he took in her state of undress and the vulnerability of her state of mind.

"Kattalvitz! See if you can find covering for the commander and then get the process rolling for getting Drake Traitor back to the Pleiades and before the High Counsel. The Free Spirit is in no shape to traverse the return trip back home, so she will need to be towed, at least until you reach the Pleiadian Quadrant. Once there, Captain Marina will be capable of maneuvering the ship on the final leg of our destination. Be sure the Free Spirit is anchored securely. We want to be sure there are no surprises as we enter the black hole on our way out of this God forsaken galaxy."

At that moment, Drake Traitor laughed wickedly aloud. All eyes turned to the man positioned between the two guards who would be responsible for guarding him until he could be put before the High

Counsel. "Ah-h-h, I see I once again have your undivided attention. You think it will be easy to deliver me to the dogs you people quiver before? Well I'm elated to tell you it won't be that easy. You continue to underestimate me Ashzar old friend." Drake Traitor threw back his head and laughed again in triumphant glee. "You honestly believe I didn't have an alternative plan in case things somehow should go awry? Ashzar, Ashzar. You let a whore cloud your judgment! You will all die in the Nississoo Galaxy! And I will enjoy the discontentment of your being here while I find a way out of this mess you and that Bitch have created. So you shut down the crystal and you think you took away my power, but, in shutting down the crystal you also wiped out the mathematical equation that made going back through the black hole possible. To get back through the black hole you will need the exact mathematical force of energy and only "I" know what it is." Drake Traitor laughed uproariously. "So you see…..in actuality I still have power over you and that disgusting piece of whore flesh you call a woman. Take me before the High Counsel? Condemn me to a judgment of Hell by those morons? No! It is I who will pass judgment and it is I who will condemn you to this Hell of never, never land." Drake Traitor looked at Ashzar's guards and said mockingly, "Take me away kind sirs. I want to savor my unmatched cleverness. Ashzar, I will be waiting for you to beg me for the equation. Better yet, send Jana to me. Perhaps she can put me in a better mood to negotiate." Drake Traitor turned to walk out of the room with the intent to leave Ashzar and Jana with the look of total shock that had registered on their faces.

Ashzar was quick to recover, however, and the sound of his voice was as the sound of all the Universes, exploding simultaneously, causing Jana to cringe inwardly at the tone. Never in all her long life had she ever heard Ashzar respond so forcibly to anything, no matter what the situation. She knew Drake Traitor had pushed to far this time and she hoped Ashzar would not, in one instant, destroy all that she loved so much about him and all the prestige that he'd worked his entire life to attain. Murderous rage glittered dangerously in his eyes where just seconds ago they'd been filled with such softness; such love.

"You pitiful, disgusting, sorry excuse of a mongrel! How dare you insult the woman of my heart; my life! How dare you think to manipulate my intelligence as High Commanding Officer of the Pleiades Star Fleet! What do you take me for...a sniveling, inexperienced child without an ounce of confidence in the powers of the Universe? A gutless, fear laden mutant of the Reptilian Cluster Experiential Expeditions? A second class unintelligent being created in the failed creations of existence along side you? You sorry son of a galactic she dog outcast! What makes you think I care about your mathematical equations? YOU, who could never hold a nickel to the likes of the Universal Equations that I've created and discarded in the wake of all that is good and Holy to uphold the laws of purity and grace! Hear me and hear me good Traitor. We WILL get through that black hole if I have to recreate it myself! And I pray that the High Counsel will allow me to dissipate the energies of your black Soul! Guards! Get this, this, thing from beyond my vision before I forget my oath to the forces of light and succumb to an action I will regret for the rest of my sojourn of this existence."

Drake Traitor was visibly shaken as the guards led him away. Jana watched as Ashzar paced back and forth, eyes closed in an effort to put the reins on his emotions and to calm himself down. All tiredness was put aside as she needed to rise to the demand of the occasion here, now, and "rise" she did. "Ashzar," Jana walked over to him and placing her arms around his waist, laid her head upon his chest. "Ashzar, I love you. I am here for you and I will always be here for you in the future whenever you need me." She stroked his hair, reveling in the feel of the thickness of it. She placed both hands on his face and looked lovingly into his eyes. She watched as the anger receded to be replaced by another emotion. Desire. Raw Desire. Jana didn't back away. She didn't want to. This was right. She knew now that this was the way it was supposed to be all along. Funny how this scenario seemed so familiar, as if they'd been in this exact time frame once before. Jana stood on her toes to place a heartfelt kiss upon Ashzar's lips. Softly at first, then much more urgently, all the hunger within her manifesting itself upon the lips of this man. "Meld with me Ash, right here. Now. Please." Copulation on the 5th Dimension was altogether different from that of Earth; it wasn't base, but the satisfaction was 1,000's of times better than that of Human fulfillment. To meld was to blend totally, thru the eyes - the windows of the soul, the heart - the seat of the soul, and the Aura - the intermingling of the soul.

Ashzar thought his heart would explode. Jana didn't need to ask twice. He'd waited his whole long life for this moment, but he knew that universal law demanded that melding, two becoming one, must be of mutual consent. One must never disobey the law of "Free Will." Ashzar swept her off her feet, and then laid her down gently as if handling a very rare piece of precious porcelain. He placed his hand upon her heart; she placed her hand on his. He claimed her mouth and Jana thought she would die of pure pleasure, but true pleasure was yet to come. Ashzar set a course when once started; nothing would have prevented him from following the lead of his emotions.

Ashzar knew she was about to take flight, but he was not about to let that happen without him being right there beside her. There was the sound of thunder, like a herd of stallions trampling the prairies on Earth's finest terrains. Together they took flight and soared to places no one else would ever tread upon. They heard laughter, they saw angels, they heard trumpets, they saw brilliant lights and they became a part of every imaginable note of music ever composed by any sentient being ever created. No one would ever top the feelings they created on this day! Descending from unheard of heights, both declared their love and lay spent within each other's arms.

Jana stirred first, awakening Ashzar in the process. He pushed the hair from her face and gathered her in his arms. "We've much to do Jana, but with you "willingly" by my side, there's nothing we can't accomplish. I love you more than you could possibly know." Jana looked at him with a smile on her lips. "I love you too Ash. Always have. I was just too stubborn to admit it, even to myself."

Someone coughed and when they looked up, Kattalvitz moved nervously from one foot to the other. "Ah, sorry Sir. Ah, the shuttle is ready to, ah, leave sir whenever you are. Ah, something for the Commander Jana, Sir. Ah," Kattalvitz was desperately trying to extricate himself from the situation he'd found himself in...."I'll just leave now sir." Face crimson, he made a mad dash for the door. Ashzar laughed while, embarrassed, Jana buried her head in his chest. "We'll be right along Kattalvitz," Ashzar called after his departing 3rd in command. Looking down at Jana he stroked her back and sighed. "Kattalvitz brought something for cover for you. Maybe if that'd been done sooner….." He chuckled. Jana smiled as the two of them arose to the demand of their stations. Covering herself with the Jumpsuit that was brought to her, they walked arm in arm in the direction of the shuttle bay. There was much to do, but from this day forward, they'd do it together.

EPILOGUE

Ashzar and Jana stood before the Pleiadian High Counsel to recant the How's and Why's and the Final outcome of the long ago missing "Lemurian Crystal." When asked how they came to be on a mission that had not been approved by the High Counsel, Ashzar offered an answer.

"Jana is a sensitive much like myself. She was able to see the Lemurian Crystal in the hands of Drake Traitor through a vision. It had been, up to now, very hard for her to get her Father or myself to listen to her views, thoughts or findings due to the fact that so many other pressing matters were always before us. Because of my oath to High councilman Dakkar to protect his daughter, Jana has always been sent on assignment as my double. She knew that I would not sway from my Mission and she also knew that her father would back my decision 100% being that I am the Senior Commander of the Star Fleet and my records speak for themselves as to the trust he places in me. However, an immediate important decision had to be made regarding the Danger the Lemurian Crystal presented in the hands of an unstable sentient being, even when that sentient being happened to be one of our own. There was no time for theories or debate. The Pleiadian Quadrant, its people and the Whole Universe was in grave danger and that danger needed to be annihilated at all cost; Stat. The level of Priority was higher than any other mission in the Information Tele-cast system.

Sirs, Jana gambled with her stature as Commander of the Free Spirit, she understood she could lose all, but took the risk because of her love for her people and those she's come to love throughout the known Universes. I had no choice but to follow, and Jana knew this, due to my oath to her Father. Once I understood the source of her disobeying my order to be aboard my Command Ship bound for earth, I too realized there was no other choice than to locate Traitor and to do everything within my power to bring Traitor to justice and to return the most powerful Energy inducer to its proper abode. That danger is now past and I hope you will agree with me that Jana deserves credit in rising to the demand of her station and Title.

Jana Stood there listening to Ashzar's elegant summation of the events from beginning to end. Not once did he speak an untruth. His defense of her actions made her heart swell and she was proud that she loved this man and he loved her in return. She looked at him as he finished and raised an eyebrow; question marks visible in her light filled eyes. Ashzar glanced at Jana and she just wanted to wrap her arms around him, or challenge him to a race or kiss him until his face was beat red. Her adrenaline was pumping and she truly needed to release the energy. She looked back to the High Counsel. They were speaking to her now and she hoped she'd caught the entire line of questioning. "Is this the way things transpired Commander Jana." Jana decided to take the cautious approach. "It is as Commander Ashzar spoke."

"Then we honor you both, Commander Jana and Commander Ashzar. It will be so noted in your Command records. Are there any other concerns that need discussing before we move on to the next assignment? They both said "Yes" at the same time and their eyes met and held for a split second. Ashzar took the lead again and addressed Dakkar. "High Councilman Dakkar. I seek your permission for your Daughter's hand and feel confident that your blessing will be upon us. Dakkar stood up from his high perch on the council bench and came down to stand before Jana and Ashzar.

"Are you both in agreement and sure that your decision is final." His eyes glinted with approval as the two said, "yes, our decision is final." Dakkar took Ashzar's hand and placed it over Jana's and said, "You are now One, and with this declaration comes my blessings."

Jana asked her Father, "Does this mean that I can now take separate missions without Commander Ashzar, Father?" Ashzar smiled

CPSIA information can be obtained at www.ICGtesting.com
Printed in the USA
LVOW080254210313

325326LV00001B/63/A

for he knew she still had a maverick side to her personality, which he loved about her, but he also knew what Dakkar's answer would be.

Dakkar looked at Jana and said simply, "No, Jana. It does not." Jana grinned at Ashzar and then looking at her father, bowed and said, "It will be as you wish."

Seated again upon the Bench with the other council members, Dakkar stated, "It is now time to move on to other important matters. The council will determine the action to be taken against Drake Traitor. We are a Quadrant of love and wish only to impose those lessons necessary to lead back to the path of light, those whose Free Will caused them to go astray, but that is not to be of your concern. What is to be of concern to you is Planet Earth. She is in the throes of her last, shall we say, Hoorah! The weeds are being separated from the wheat as we speak and our Fleet shall make ready to intervene at the exact moment that the Prince of Light receives approval from his/our Father/Mother Supreme Creator. In the meantime, while the many ships wait in orbit surrounding Earth Shan, continue to try to get those who still slumber to awaken and to take seriously their Free Will choices to join us here in the light or to be confined to the path of darkness. Remember, you can only intervene if you are asked. Hopefully, many will realize, before it is too late, that there is no such thing as separateness, but that all are contained in the one. The mission is to be carried out immediately. So be it.

Jana and Ashzar bowed, turned on their heels and left the council room. Outside of the room they walked Arm in Arm, contentment on their faces towards Ashzar's Command Ship. Jana looked up at Ashzar and said, "Thank you Ash. Your explanation back there could have been decidedly different." Ashzar grinned and said, "What and lose the most beautiful, stubborn, mischievous, exasperating woman on the Pleiades?" He bent his head and kissed her long and hard. "Let's go Jana love, we've got a lot of hard work ahead of us. Earth awaits................